CRIME CLASSICS

Tim Frazer
Again

Also in the Crime Classics series:

MY FRIEND MR CAMPION AND OTHER MYSTERIES
Margery Allingham

BLUEPRINT FOR MURDER
Roger Bax

DEATH WALKS IN EASTREPPS
THE NORWICH VICTIMS
Francis Beeding

TRIAL AND ERROR
Anthony Berkeley

THE PYTHON PROJECT
THE WHIP HAND
Victor Canning

MY BROTHER'S KILLER
THE SLEEPING TIGER
Dominic Devine

BAT OUT OF HELL
THE TYLER MYSTERY
THE WORLD OF TIM FRAZER
Francis Durbridge

ALL THE LONELY PEOPLE
YESTERDAY'S PAPERS
Martin Edwards

THE CASE OF THE CROOKED CANDLE
Eric Stanley Gardner

NO TEARS FOR HILDA
Andrew Garve

BEFORE THE FACT
Francis Ilesy

THROUGH A GLASS, DARKLY
Helen McCloy

JOHNNY UNDER GROUND
WHO SAW HER DIE?
Patricia Moyes

CLOSE UP ON DEATH
Maureen O'Brien

LONELY MAGDALEN
Henry Wade

SOME MUST WATCH
Ethel Lina White

Tim Frazer Again

A TIM FRAZER THRILLER

FRANCIS DURBRIDGE

ABOUT THE AUTHOR

Francis Durbridge (1912-1998), had a brief career as a stockbroker's clerk before success with a radio-play encouraged him to become a full-time writer. Most famous as the creator of Paul Temple, Durbridge also wrote a trilogy of thrillers featuring Tim Frazer, an engineer who is gradually recruited by a secret government department as an undercover agent. Like the Temple series, the Tim Frazer stories were adapted for television, running for eighteen episodes.

This edition published in the UK by Arcturus Publishing Limited
26/27 Bickels Yard, 151–153 Bermondsey Street, London SE1 3HA

Design and layout copyright © 2013 Arcturus Publishing Limited
Text copyright © The Estate of Francis Durbridge, 1972

Cover artwork by Steve Beaumont
Typesetting by Couper Street Type Co.

AD003691EN

Printed in the UK

CHAPTER ONE

I

When I reached the end of the mews and saw the line of traffic, I realised that the rush hour was at its height. Four taxis crawled past, their drivers staring obstinately ahead. My appointment with Mr. Ross was for six. It meant that precisely. I glanced at my watch, saw that it was barely five-thirty, and decided to walk.

As I wended my way towards Smith Square I wondered what Charles Ross had in store for me. He hadn't been any more communicative than usual on the telephone. When I'd asked what my next assignment was he'd replied, somewhat curtly, 'The Salinger affair – if that conveys anything to you.'

It hadn't, of course, and I'd hung up on a dead line, wondering what kind of a fool I was to have let myself be caught up in the cloak and dagger business of a Government department that was a cross between M.I.5 and the C.I.D. I should have gone back to engineering and had fun and games with shop stewards over tea breaks.

Searching frantically for Harry Denston – my ex-partner, whose extravagance had sent our engineering business into liquidation – I had suddenly come into close contact with Charles Ross and his Merrie Men. Ross was also looking for my ex-partner and, realising that my knowledge of Harry and his associates might prove more than useful, he had enlisted my help and put the full resources of his department at my disposal.

I caught up with Harry eventually, discovering in the process that I had an hitherto unsuspected streak of ruthlessness in my make-up. To be honest with myself, my conceit was flattered when Ross offered me a position on the staff of his department. Perhaps if I'd been married . . . But I wasn't. As Big Ben boomed out the first stroke of six I turned into Smith Square.

2

As I was ushered into the room I thought, as I always had, how improbable a setting it was for the briefing of a mission that could well culminate in violent death. It was high and spacious, with an Adam ceiling, a veined marble mantelpiece, and wall-fitted bookcases. Several club leather easy chairs were strategically placed on the thick, fitted carpet. The only reminders that you hadn't been invited for a social visit were the steel filing cabinet in one corner and the four businesslike telephones on the period desk.

Behind the desk sat a man in his early fifties, neatly groomed and wearing an inconspicuous, well fitting dark grey suit. At a first glance he might have been mistaken for a successful businessman; it was not until he started to speak that you realised Charles Ross possessed certain qualities which would have been wasted in the world of commerce.

He rose as I came in, gave me his deceptively benevolent smile, and shook hands. As he sat down again he inclined his head towards a man sprawled in one of the leather easy chairs.

'I want you to meet Lewis Richards, Frazer. He'll be a colleague of yours on this case.' He shot an amused glance at the other man. 'He's not entirely sold that we have a case at all. Or is your cynicism just a cover for laziness, Richards?'

Richards smiled sardonically. 'Weariness, sir. Wasn't it Bernard Shaw who said you need Alpine boots to tramp round the art galleries? How that woman covered so much ground in stiletto heels will always be a mystery to me.' He stood up and took my hand in a firm grip. 'Do you know how many museums there are in Amsterdam, Frazer?'

I smiled blankly in the way you do to that sort of question, and he sank back in his chair.

'You will,' he assured me.

I gave him an appraising glance. He had an intelligent face, with a long, shrewd nose. His brown eyes had the good-humoured tolerance of having seen everything and not believing half of it. I had a feeling I was going to get along with my new colleague.

Ross said brusquely: 'This is a photograph of the woman you will be having under observation, Frazer.' He took a print from his blotter and handed it to me.

It was a photograph of a woman in her early thirties. A brunette, with wide-spaced dark eyes, a well-shaped nose, and a full, generous mouth. I could have thought of many less pleasant assignments than trailing legs as slender as those below the knee-length sheath skirt.

'Her name is Barbara Day,' Ross was saying. 'She's English. Part owner of an antique business in Kensington. She's engaged to a stockbroker. A man named Arthur Fairlee.'

I glanced up over the photograph to catch Richards' satirical gaze. 'Lucky man, Fairlee. Eh, Frazer?'

Ross cut in abruptly. 'She's flying to Amsterdam the day after tomorrow. I've arranged for you to travel on the same plane.' He looked at me. 'You've brought your passport?'

I produced the passport. Ross gave it a quick glance and pushed it into a drawer.

'It will be returned to you before you leave.'

It seemed high time I asked a leading question, so I said: 'May I ask why you want this woman kept under observation, sir?'

Ross took a cigarette from a silver box and pushed the box across to my side of his desk. 'Just over six weeks ago an agent of this department called Leo Salinger was killed. He was knocked down by a car driven by Barbara Day.'

I helped myself to a cigarette. 'You suspect it wasn't an accident – is that it?'

Richards made a steeple of his forefingers and thumbs, gazing through it, one eye screwed up. 'That's the loaded question, Frazer.'

Ross snapped off his lighter in the direction of Richards with a half smile. 'Well, let's put it this way. Leo was one of our best men. There must have been several people who wanted him out of the way.'

I wondered, a trifle uneasily, whether I'd ever achieve that unenviable status in the department. 'But there'd be an inquest. Didn't anything come out in the evidence?'

Ross nodded across at Richards. 'You take over, Richards. You were there.'

'It was a genuine enough accident, according to the witnesses,' Richards said heavily. 'They said Barbara Day did her best to pull up, but just didn't have a chance to avoid Salinger. According to their testimony he stepped off the pavement right in front of the car.'

I glanced again at the open, attractive face in the photograph. 'Any idea what Barbara Day was doing in Amsterdam at the time?'

Ross cut in: 'We know she was there on holiday.'

'She's been back there since the accident?' I said.

Ross nodded. 'She flew there about six weeks ago and stayed six days. We sent Richards over to tail her.'

Richards groaned hollowly. 'Six days of museums and art galleries. And nothing more incriminating to report than a sidelong glance at a male nude statue.'

I smiled. 'And yet you still suspect her of not being entirely innocent of causing Salinger's death?'

'Not me,' Richards said emphatically. 'For my part, it was a pure accident. These things happen . . . even to us.' He pulled at his long nose. 'Only I can't convince Mr. Ross that's all it was.'

'All right, Richards,' Ross said soothingly. 'I know you think I've a bee in my bonnet about Miss Day. But there it is.'

Richards laughed embarrassedly. 'I didn't say that, sir.'

'I wouldn't hold it against you if you had.' Ross smiled at him paternally, then his face tightened as he turned to me. 'These trips back to Holland by Miss Day can't be completely purposeless. I want to know what their significance is. That's your assignment, Frazer. I want a report from you on everyone she meets and where she goes.' He rotated his cigarette lightly between finger and thumb. 'I'd particularly like to know whether she visits a café called *De Kroon*.'

I raised my eyebrows. 'Why *De Kroon* particularly?'

'Salinger used to frequent it.' Ross opened a side drawer in his desk and brought out a street map of Amsterdam. Spreading it out on the desk he put a manicured finger on a red-encircled street name. 'Keizersgracht Platz. *De Kroon*'s is just round the corner.'

I made a mental note of it. 'Salinger,' I said. 'Can you tell me anything about him? What was he doing in Holland?'

'He lived there. Worked in Amsterdam. From time to time he supplied us with information.'

Ross's mouth tightened, so I did not press the obvious question about the nature of the information. Instead, I queried: 'Did anyone know about this?'

He shook his head slowly. 'Not that we are aware of. But, of course, certain people must have known we had a contact in Holland and that information was coming through to us.' He smiled thinly. 'Nothing you need concern yourself about. Just information about things in general.'

You perceptive old devil, I thought. I said, 'What if Richards is right? That the accident was genuine and Miss Day wasn't interested in Salinger?'

Ross gave me a long, cold-eyed stare. 'I ask the questions, Frazer. Your job is to bring me the answers. Your plane ticket to Amsterdam will be mailed to you tonight.'

I didn't need cueing to know what my next line was. 'Good-bye, sir.'

As I passed Richards' chair he hooded one eye at me. 'I hope you like museums, Frazer,' he said softly.

I came out of the house into the gathering darkness of the evening. Opposite me, in the centre of the square, was the bombed-out church with its four-cornered spires. They said Queen Anne had kicked over a footstool and told her architects to build a church like it. I felt a lot of sympathy for those architects. My instructions didn't seem to make a great deal more sense.

CHAPTER TWO

The plane ticket arrived the next morning, together with the altered passport. I was relieved to find that I wouldn't be travelling under an assumed name. Ross had simply changed my occupation. It now read 'Journalist' instead of 'Engineer'. A typed note inside the passport said: 'You are commissioned to write articles for a trade paper. Engineering stuff as you know the lingo. Take a cine-camera with you. And use it. Destroy this.' It bore no signature. It didn't need to; Charles Ross's personality was stamped all over it.

The following morning I was at the Air Terminal well ahead of bus departure time. I hung around the bookstall, keeping an eye on the stairway up to the lounge.

When she did come I drew a quick breath. Her photograph hadn't flattered her. She was hatless, and her raven-black hair was cut short and combed in a fringe round her ears and forehead. It suited her neat-shaped head. She had a fur coat draped across her shoulders, over a dark suit; and her legs looked as though they'd stepped straight out of a stocking advertisement. Even if I hadn't been on an assignment I'd have been watching her every movement with . . . well, interest.

As she came beside me at the bookstall a faint perfume I couldn't put a name to accompanied her. I felt like a bloodhound who'd been given a glove to sniff and told to follow that scent. If I'd had a tail I'd have wagged it

She bought a *Harper's Bazaar* and the last of Laurence Durrell's quartet. She had a quiet, low voice that must have made Arthur Fairlee's day when she telephoned him.

I let her board the bus ahead of me, then found an empty seat three rows away on the opposite side of the aisle.

Just as we were about to leave, a latecomer came panting towards the bus and scrambled aboard. He was obviously an American; he wore a panama hat, striped shirt, a check suit, and a gaily coloured tie. Yet there was nothing brash about him as he came in waving his airways zipper bag and favouring all and sundry with a shy grin. He took the one vacant seat, next to Barbara Day.

He seemed to be on easy conversational terms with her before we reached that long, boring stretch of the Great West Road, and I felt vaguely envious. He was about my own age, I judged, though he was obviously cultivating a more youthful appearance than his years.

When we reached the airport I was first out of the coach and into the reception hall. On the tarmac I was way ahead of the other passengers. I waited for Barbara Day to mount the gangway, then followed her into the aircraft. As I half hesitated beside her double seat she looked up and smiled at me.

'Oh . . . I'm terribly sorry. Are these in your way?'

She reached out and collected her handbag, magazine, and book from the place beside hers.

As I seated myself and thanked her the doors of the plane closed. From the back the calm, aloof voice of the air hostess reminded us not to smoke, and to fasten our safety belts.

When we were airborne and had released our safety belts I produced my cigarette case and, after a momentary hesitation, held it out to her. She took one with a slim-fingered hand, the nails crimson and a trifle too elongated for my liking. Not that I could fault her otherwise. After I'd lit both our cigarettes and she'd tucked the magazine and book beside her I mentally scored myself a few points up on Richards. From what I'd gathered he'd trailed her the hard way, lurking behind newspapers as he'd tramped after her through museums and art galleries. Then suddenly I felt a moment of misgiving. After all, Richards was an old hand; yet he chose to keep out of sight of his quarry. Could there be some flaw in my own tactics? Would I find myself in a situation I couldn't handle?

A quarter of an hour before we were due to land I felt bound to create an opening that might lead to some clue as to the purpose of her journey.

'Why anyone comes to Holland for a holiday defeats me,' I said off-handedly. 'Only a business trip would drag me here.'

'That could be Arthur, my fiancé, talking,' she said with mild exasperation. 'Mention holidays to him and he immediately thinks of the South of France'

'At least you can be sure of the sun there,' I said urbanely. 'I suppose Holland has its points. But the weather's usually foul.'

'Oh, nonsense! I've been to Holland several times and the weather's been marvellous.'

'You've been very lucky, that's all I can say.' I pushed it as far as I dared without arousing her suspicions. 'What's the attraction when the tulips aren't in bloom?'

'Windmills.' Her eyes mocked me for a moment. 'Oh, well – just to satisfy your curiosity! It's the museums and art galleries. Amsterdam is the city of museums, you know.' As though to emphasise that the attraction wasn't male she played with her engagement ring, then quickly changed the subject. 'So you're on a business trip?'

I nodded. 'I'm a journalist. I write technical articles. Mostly on engineering subjects. That's the reason I'm going to Amsterdam. They've got hold of a new technique in steel outer walling that my trade paper's interested in.'

'Rather outside my province, I'm afraid,' she said, smiling. 'Hello . . . I think we're coming in to land.'

Almost immediately the Captain's voice came over the intercom informing us that we were due in at Schipol Airport in a few minutes' time, and would we fasten our seat belts, please? 'The weather in Amsterdam,' he added, 'is fine and sunny.'

Barbara Day wrinkled her nose at me. 'There . . . you see?' She opened her handbag, brought out a mirror, and began to do unnecessary things to her face. Presently she said, over a lipstick: 'Thanks for helping to pass the time so pleasantly. Perhaps we'll run into one another in Amsterdam.'

Smiling, I hoped not too ironically, I said: 'I'll look out for you.'

The plane nosed down towards the flat Holland coastline. Away to the left the spires of Amsterdam were silhouetted against the blue sky of a perfect spring afternoon. Crisscrossing the city, like white ribbons, were the canals. In the sunshine, Amsterdam's claim to be the Venice of the North seemed less of a travel brochure's extravaganza than is usually the case.

I let Barbara Day precede me through the Passport Control and Customs. Here, instead of having her smart blue and yellow striped suitcase put on the airline bus trolley she picked it up and walked quickly to the main exit. I grabbed my own case from the trolley and hurried after her, arriving at the exit just in time to see a sheer-nylon sheathed leg disappear into a taxi. I signalled the next in the rank but lost it to the American. From his gesticulations with the zipper bag I had the impression he was instructing the driver to follow the other cab.

A moment later I was going through the same performance myself. Luckily my driver knew enough English to get the idea quickly. With a cheroot wagging from his lips he said, 'Certainly, sir,' in a flat, expressionless voice.

In Amsterdam we followed the other taxis along a busy street beside a canal. As we approached the most impressive of its many bridges the cabs we were following slowed and drew in to the kerb. Leaning forward, I told my driver to carry on past them. 'Okay, sir,' he called back as I ducked down to avoid being recognised by the woman and the man who were now on the pavement, exchanging surprised greetings.

At the next corner I stopped my taxi, and as I paid off the driver I thought some light-hearted comment on the situation was called for. There was always a chance that he might report the incident to the police, and then I'd have a plainclothes man on *my* tail. So I mumbled something about a pretty girl on the plane and wanting to find out where she was staying. I needn't have bothered. All it got me was a shrugged, 'Why not?' and, as I discovered later, an Austrian schilling among my change.

I went down the street that ran at right angles to the canal until I came to a small hotel. It wouldn't rate a single star in a Michelin hotel guide. But the red-bricked floor of Reception was freshly polished and you could see your face in the metal surface of the massive stove.

They gave me a room, austerely furnished but spotlessly clean, overlooking the street. It was next door to a bathroom and, after I'd unpacked my shirts and the one other suit I'd brought, I took a quick shower. When I'd dressed I went out and bought a street guide.

In an unpretentious bar I thumbed through the guide, and took my bearings from one of the maps. Eventually I found the Keizersgracht Platz without much difficulty, and I memorised the route to it from my present position. Then I paid for my lager and went out to give *De Kroon*'s a looking over.

It was a typical Continental restaurant, with tables on the pavement in brave defiance of the Dutch climate. I'd always found the trick is to watch the customers at the outside tables before you decide to enter. If they look like locals, and there are no camera-slung tourists among them, you can be pretty sure the food will be good and the charges reasonable. *De Kroon*'s passed the test. However, I did not go inside.

I rambled around for a couple of hours, still getting my bearings. A mist drifted in from the sea, and since I badly needed a drink and some food to take the chill out of my bones I decided to return to the Keizersgracht Platz. It was splattered with neon-lit bars and restaurants. I was too eager to get into somewhere to be choosey, so I turned into the first revolving door I came to.

What little atmosphere the restaurant possessed was laid on for the tourist trade. Waitresses in national costume with blonde plaits draped over their shoulders; a chef in international costume, grinning with false bonhomie behind a charcoal grill; a long bar with a bartender who'd have answered to 'Harry' in any tourist-haunted bar from Paris to Rome. Just to be in on the act I flung back a couple of Dutch gins in rapid succession, then, feeling like a refuelled dragon, sat down at a table.

After the gin the menu was overcrowded and elusive, so I settled for the house speciality, a dish called Runderlappen. Runderlappen turned out to be stewed steak, but rather better than Mother makes. By the time I had a cognac in front of me and a cigarette alight I felt able to give some thought to my first day's trailing of Barbara Day.

So far, I was inclined to agree with Richards. She'd discussed herself quite freely on the plane – mentioned her interest in an antique business and referred to her fiancé with the naturalness of a girl who had nothing to hide. I thought about Arthur Fairlee. A stockbroker seemed an unlikely fiancé for a girl who was mixed up with the kind of people that Ross's department was interested in. I sipped my cognac. Arthur Fairlee was a damned lucky chap!

I returned to the conversation on the plane. She hadn't

shown the slightest evasiveness when I'd questioned her about her frequent visits to Amsterdam. Or had she? Abruptly, I stubbed out my cigarette, remembering how she'd evaded the subject when I'd pushed my questioning almost to the point of rudeness. I lit another cigarette and expelled the smoke from my lungs ceilingwards. That was it. She'd turned the conversation to what *I* was doing in Amsterdam as a riposte to my own boorish inquisitiveness.

A man's voice, ordering a round of drinks, suddenly reminded me of the American. Where did he fit into the picture? He could be a lot less the innocent tourist than he looked. In which case, there were two of us trailing Barbara Day. Alternatively, there might be no more to it than the usual reason why a man chases an attractive girl. Not relishing either of my half-baked conclusions, and the last one the least, I paid my bill and went back to my hotel.

CHAPTER THREE

I

Four days later I was sitting in the window of a café opposite a museum. By this time I had worked out a method of procedure for keeping Barbara Day under observation. After following her at a discreet distance around five museums I decided that my conscience would be satisfied if I simply watched her go into a museum and then consumed two or three lagers at a nearby café until she came out. Maybe Richards would not have approved, but his more scrupulous method had brought no better result.

Apart from that, I'd discovered that trailing Miss Day was another word for boredom. I'd compiled a list of where she'd been apart from her visits to places of historic interest. Shops, cinemas, restaurants – the lot. She hadn't been within a quarter mile of *De Kroon*'s.

As I watched her stroll out of the museum I gulped down my beer with the decisiveness of a man of action. That afternoon I would contact Barbara Day and risk the consequences.

At two o'clock I was outside her hotel, mixing with the crowds and, not to make too obvious my interest in the door of the hotel, occasionally going through the motions of photographing the pleasure craft passing to and fro on the canal.

She didn't show up until three. Then she came briskly out of the hotel, crossed the road, went down the steps beside the bridge, and boarded a pleasure craft.

When it had moved off I went down on to the landing stage and checked the timetable there. The boat was due to return at four. That gave me an hour to waste. I put in time over a couple of beers in a nearby pavement café.

On the dot of four I stationed myself at the top of the steps leading to the landing stage, and as her boat drew in I put the cine-camera to my eye. This time the film was purring. It should have been colour film; the plain red dress was a perfect contrast to her dark loveliness.

I dropped the camera on to my chest as she came up the steps. It wasn't until I said, 'Good afternoon,' that she noticed me. Her lips parted, then her surprise melted into a warm smile.

'Oh, hello there!' she exclaimed, gesturing a greeting with a black-gloved hand.

'Still alone, I see.'

'And loving every moment of it! No one to please but myself.'

'What are you doing in this part of the town?' I asked innocently. 'Don't tell me you've run out of art galleries?'

She shook her head. 'I thought I'd rest from art galleries and museums this afternoon.'

She came and stood beside me, gazing down at the water. 'It's lovely, isn't it?' she said presently, with a sigh of contentment.

At that moment I couldn't think of anything more perfect. 'You're right about Holland. It's got something.'

She glanced up at me gratefully. It was with an effort that

I forced myself to lead into the object for our seemingly casual meeting. 'By the way, what do you do with yourself in the evenings?'

She shrugged. 'Oh, nothing very exciting. Find somewhere to eat, usually. There are some very nice little restaurants in Amsterdam.'

'There certainly are,' I said, with a great show of enthusiasm. 'I found a delightful place last night. *De Kroon.*' I glanced at her quickly. 'Do you know it?'

She frowned perplexedly. '*De Kroon?*'

I nodded, without taking my eyes from her face.

'No, I don't,' she said slowly. 'I don't think I've heard of it. Where is it, exactly?'

It sounded like the truth. But I decided to maintain my outward enthusiasm, hoping I might still trap her into an involuntary lapse. 'You go into the Dolderplatz and turn right at the Keizersgracht . . . Sorry . . . I mean you go into the Keizersgracht and turn right at the Dolderplatz, then through the Middlestrasse and turn left . . .' I swallowed, and started again. 'Look – you turn left at the Middlestrasse, then when you get to the Keizersgracht . . .'

'Oh, do stop,' she implored laughingly, putting a hand on my arm. 'You obviously haven't the slightest idea where it is.'

I grinned sheepishly. 'We could take a taxi there.' I snapped my fingers. 'I say, that's an idea! Why not let me take you there now, for a drink?'

For a moment she gazed down at a swan floating along the canal. Then she said slowly: 'It's awfully kind of you – but

I have to go back to the hotel to change for dinner. I'm going to . . .'

I cut in on her. 'That's all right. There's loads of time to fit in a drink. How about meeting me here in an hour?'

'Well,' she began hesitantly, then with a quick smile she glanced at her watch. 'Thank you very much. I'll take you up on that. I'll see you back here at five-thirty, if that's all right with you?'

'Splendid!' I exclaimed with unfeigned pleasure. 'Five-thirty it is. 'Bye now.' I cocked an eyebrow at her. 'And don't go wandering off to a museum!'

She turned away, laughing. 'I won't.'

With an odd feeling of light-heartedness I watched her cross the road to her hotel. I was sure now that the name *De Kroon* had been no more significant to her than if I'd mentioned a restaurant in Timbuctoo. Ross had got his lines crossed where Barbara Day was concerned. That was the way I wanted it to be.

2

There was a lot of warmth still left in the sun when we arrived at *De Kroon*'s. The place was crowded at that hour, but a discreetly displayed tip had persuaded a waiter there was room for one more table outside.

After I'd ordered a cinzano for my companion and a dry martini for myself I went out onto the pavement and started to take some cine-camera shots of the colourful scene.

I was focusing the camera on Barbara Day when I suddenly realised she was talking to someone. A second later a man's figure came into my viewfinder.

'Hello there!' exclaimed a familiar voice. It was the American, the same disarming grin on his slightly chubby features.

I lowered the camera and managed to wipe the scowl off my face as he embarked upon a detailed account of his day's adventures. Slowly, I went back to the table. He was beaming at Barbara Day so agreeably that it was impossible to feel annoyed.

'Have I been around!' he exclaimed. 'I've just about walked my feet to the bone buying things for the folks back home.'

'Of course, you're going back tomorrow.' She nodded. Then, as my shadow fell across the table, she turned to introduce us.

He stuck out a massive hand. 'Glad to know you, sir,' he exclaimed, and sounded as if he really meant it. I did my best to reciprocate, but it was an effort.

'Mr. Cordwell is staying at my hotel,' Barbara Day told me.

He nodded eagerly. 'And we're always bumping into each other outside the hotel. In boats, buses, elevators . . .'

'Museums?' I interrupted, a trifle maliciously.

'No, *sir*!' Cordwell pawed the air contemptuously. 'No museums. Not for me!' His hand dropped to the back of a chair. 'Say, do you mind if I take the weight off my feet . . . ?'

I accepted the inevitable. 'Of course not.'

'I don't wish to intrude . . .'

I bit back the short answer to that one, and said: 'No . . . no, that's quite all right.'

He planted his zipper bag on the table, put his camera underneath it, and deposited himself in the vacant chair. 'That's better. Europe's a great place, Mr. Frazer. I really go for it. But my feet! Will they be glad to be back home!'

I gave him his laugh, stuffed my camera back in its case, and laid it down resignedly. Just for something to say, I asked: 'Is this your first visit to Holland, Mr. Cordwell?'

'No, indeed. I was here about five or six weeks ago. Did the whole country in two days. Didn't figure on coming back.' He rubbed a hand over his crew cut. 'But I had a rather unfortunate experience.'

I raised my eyebrows politely. 'What was that?'

'The night I was leaving, someone broke into my hotel room and lifted my baggage.' He grinned ruefully. 'Well, not just my baggage. They stole everything – literally everything.'

Barbara Day glanced at him sympathetically. 'Oh, but how dreadful for you.'

'Yeah.' Cordwell beamed at her appreciatively. 'Can you imagine! I'd just got the one suit and a sports shirt . . . the things I stood up in.'

I could see he was going to make a meal of the incident, so I fed him a cue. 'What did you do? Take the next flight home?'

He gave me a grateful look. 'That's one thing the thief didn't steal from me – my vacation. I bought me a new outfit and just kept going.'

'But surely,' said Barbara Day, 'you reported your loss to the police?'

'You're darned right I did.' He leaned forward. 'And here's

the payoff. A week ago the police picked up the guy who stole my stuff and cabled me to come here and claim it. I was in London – just about to fly home. But you bet I came right back here – and fast.'

'You've had all your stuff returned, I hope?' I said.

'Everything except a pair of binoculars.'

'You're a lucky man, Mr. Cordwell.'

He shrugged. 'Glad you think so.'

'Don't get me wrong,' I said. 'I didn't mean to . . .'

He waved me down with an outsize paw. 'Forget it, Mr. Frazer. In a catastrophic sort of way I guess I was kind of lucky.' He snapped his fingers at a passing waiter. 'The same again for my two friends. And you can make mine a Scotch on the rocks.'

I could have been wrong about tourists never having discovered *De Kroon*'s. The waiter smiled imperturbably, said, 'Cinzano, dry martini, and a Scotch on the rocks,' and bustled off to the bar.

Cordwell turned back to us with an amused smile. 'Guess that guy knows how many guilders go to a dollar!' He ripped back the zipper of his bag. 'I was shopping all morning. Made some cute purchases too! Take a look at this.' He dived a hand into the bag and took out a miniature bicycle. Seated on it was a stuffed cloth doll, a Dutchman dressed in national costume. 'Ain't that something, now?'

Barbara Day's lips quivered in a slight smile. 'It's sweet.'

'Wait till I show you today's best buy. A real bargain. I bought it just along the street here.' He rummaged around the bag, not finding what he wanted. With an exasperated grunt he pulled out a bulb catalogue and threw it on the table.

I glanced at the garish cover. 'Planning to have a Dutch garden back home, Cordwell?' I asked.

'Aw, that's for my brother,' he said, then triumphantly produced an exquisitely designed metronome and placed it on the table. 'Ain't that swell? You know what they call that? A metronome. It's for musicians. Beats out the time. You just wind it up . . . like so . . .' He enjoyed himself winding it. 'Got it for my niece, Shirley. She's quite a piano player. At least, so her Mom says – I wouldn't know. I got no ear for music – not the square stuff she plays, anyway.' Flicking the pendulum, he set the metronome going, and beat time with a pudgy finger. Then he stopped, and grinned self-consciously. 'Anyhow, it *looks* good!'

'It's beautiful,' Barbara Day said breathlessly.

'Sure is! I've seen 'em back in the States, but never one like this.'

I wasn't just being polite when I said I'd never before seen one with such delicate workmanship.

Cordwell practically flapped his arms. 'I'm some picker!' he enthused. 'That must be the cutest metropole in the whole world.'

'Metronome,' Barbara Day corrected softly, her eyes smiling at me.

Cordwell offered me a cigar from a bulging case. When I'd declined he stuffed one in an outsize holder, clamped it between his teeth, and looked as happy as a child with a teat. That wasn't a bad description of his round, chubby face.

Then the waiter came with the drinks and over them we drifted into the cliché-ridden talk that passes for conversation when it's a one woman two men party.

CHAPTER FOUR

A few days later I was back at London Airport. I'd wired Ross the time of my plane's arrival – but I hadn't expected it would get me the V.I.P. treatment that it did.

As we trooped into the lounge a ground hostess stared at us questioningly. 'Mr. Frazer? Mr. Tim Frazer, please.'

I crossed to her, accompanied by stares varying between wide-eyed curiosity and yellow-eyed balefulness.

'There's a car waiting for you, Mr. Frazer,' she said briskly. 'I'm to hurry you through Passport and Customs.'

It was red carpet progress. A Customs officer had my bag and camera case chalked in a matter of seconds. I grinned at him, remembering the cross-examinations I'd been subjected to when I'd passed through Customs under my own steam. They'd even laid on a porter for me.

Outside, a black Humber Snipe was drawn up to the kerb. I had a glimpse of Ross in the back, glowering at me speculatively from under the brim of a homburg. Then a chauffeur took my bag and camera from the porter. He opened the car door, placed my luggage on the floor, and a moment later I was sitting next to Ross, listening to him saying: 'I want a quick report on Barbara Day, so that I can set the machinery going without wasting even an hour. This is urgent, Frazer.'

We were crossing the Chiswick fly-over before he'd reluctantly accepted my views on Barbara Day.

He tilted the homburg forward slightly. 'So what it really boils down to is, you agree with Richards. You think she's genuine?'

He sounded so damned disappointed that I almost wished I had something more than trivialities to tell him. 'Well, yes . . . I'm afraid I do, sir.'

He grunted. 'You watched her most of the time, I take it?'

I nodded. 'I didn't stay at the same hotel, but apart from that she was seldom out of my sight. In any case, she had most of her meals out.'

'H'm . . .' After a pause Ross said: 'What about the café I mentioned? *De Kroon*. Did she go there?'

'At my invitation. It was getting near the end of her stay and I could see she wasn't going there of her own accord. So I thought I'd take her along . . .'

Ross eased the homburg again and gave me a long, probing stare. 'Why?' he asked sharply.

I had a feeling that he'd begun to suspect my interest in Barbara Day wasn't entirely professional. 'I wanted to see if anyone would recognise her,' I said. 'The waiters, for instance.'

'And did anyone recognise her?'

'No.' Suddenly I remembered Cordwell, and wondered why I'd overlooked our meeting at the *De Kroon*. 'Well, that's not quite true,' I said lamely.

Ross ran his hand down his face despairingly. 'For God's sake, Frazer! Do I have to drag the facts out of you?'

I gave him a hurried description of Cordwell's encounters with Barbara Day.

'You really think he followed her to the hotel?'

'It looked suspiciously like it. I imagine he thought he'd made an impression.' I broke off with a little laugh, but Ross was frowning. 'Anyway, he barged in on us at *De Kroon*. We couldn't get rid of him. He went on talking for hours.'

'About what?' said Ross sharply.

'Himself mostly. Insisted on showing us his souvenirs – in between complaining about his feet. I think Barbara Day was as bored as I was.'

'Oh, yes,' Ross said with a touch of acerbity in his voice.

'There was one thing that made me curious, though.' As I said it I thought that curiosity was not exactly the word which described my feelings at the time. 'On one occasion this character addressed Miss Day by her Christian name. Of course, they'd been staying at the same hotel and had apparently run into each other from time to time – in buses, boats, and so on. But it was the way he said it. Just for an instant I had the impression they were more than . . . well . . . casual acquaintances.'

Ross rubbed his chin reflectively. 'What did he look like?'

'A typical American tourist. Looked as though he'd just stepped out of a shower. He was anything between thirty-five and forty. About my height . . . say, five-eleven. I've got him on some film I shot at *De Kroon*.'

'Has the film been processed?' Ross asked quickly.

'Not yet.' I picked up my camera. 'It's in here.'

Ross held out his hand. 'Let me have it. I'll send it down

to the lab directly I get back.' He straightened his hat. 'And I'll want you at Smith Square this afternoon. Three o'clock. We'll run the film through then.' He leaned across to the driver. 'Drop me off at Orchard Street.'

Ross settled himself back in his corner and, until we reached Orchard Street, stared unseeingly out of his side window, his fingers tapping impatiently on the camera case in his lap. I was desperately in need of a cigarette, but that would have meant offering my case to Ross, and he seemed to have entirely forgotten my presence. It suited me; I was feeling none too confident, and I didn't want a curt refusal of a proffered cigarette to remind me of my shortcomings.

After we'd dropped Ross at Orchard Street, with a laconic reminder that he expected me at three sharp, the chauffeur drove me to my mews flat.

CHAPTER FIVE

It wasn't my lucky day. There was a hold-up in Whitehall and my taxi was diverted along the Strand, then down Wellington Street, and along the Victoria Embankment.

It was ten past three when I was ushered into the library at Smith Square. The curtains had been drawn and Ross was pacing the floor, hands plunged into his jacket pockets. A small screen had been drawn down over the bookcase at one end of the room. At the other, Richards was fiddling with a projector.

Ross waved aside my apologies impatiently. 'Find yourself a chair,' he said brusquely. He swung a leg over the edge of his desk and nodded to Richards. 'All set?'

Richards reached across to the light switch, flicked it off, then started the projector.

As the preliminary blank piece of film flickered on to the screen I said: 'You'll see Barbara Day in the second shot – boarding a motor launch for a pleasure cruise. Then I took her going into a museum . . .'

I found myself staring, open mouthed, at the first sequence of shots. They were of a quiet, tree-lined square that was as unfamiliar to me as a square in Budapest.

'Hey! Just a minute,' I exclaimed when I'd caught my breath. 'This isn't my film.'

Ross's voice cut across the whirr of the projector. 'It's the film from your camera! And that's Amsterdam. I know that square well.'

'Well, I don't,' I said shortly. 'Why, I've never set eyes on that church in my life.'

Ross called abruptly: 'That'll do, Richards. Better switch on the light.'

As the projector cut out and the chandelier blazed into light Ross crossed over to me. 'Now look, Frazer, that's your film. I took the camera straight to the lab directly I got back, and waited while they developed the film.'

'I'm sorry, sir,' I said, trying to control my temper under his hostile stare. 'That isn't my film.'

'Don't contradict me, Frazer.' He smiled tightly. 'Perhaps you've forgotten about those shots. Just as seeing Cordwell at the *De Kroon* seemed to have slipped your memory this afternoon.'

I flushed. 'If that's how you feel . . .'

Richards interrupted suavely. 'Suppose we run through the rest of the film, sir? There does seem to be some – er – conflict of opinion here; maybe the rest of the film will solve the mystery.'

Ross swung round on his heel, went back to his desk, and took a cigarette from the silver box. 'All right, Richards. We'll see the complete film.'

I relaxed in my chair as the film began to roll again. And the further it went the lower my blood pressure became. One thing was certain – this wasn't my film. I recognised the Rembrandthuis only because I'd trailed Barbara Day there. I glanced over at Ross, a slight grin on my face. As I did so he stiffened and, without taking his eyes from the screen, signalled with the lighted end of his cigarette to Richards.

I looked back at the screen quickly. This was a shot of a busy shopping street. Among the crowd on the pavement, and conspicuous only because he was elbowing his way through the dawdling shoppers, was a well dressed, dapper little man. But for the untidily wrapped parcel under his arm I'd have guessed him to be a diplomat. I'd hardly registered all this when the man stepped blindly off the pavement.

I flinched automatically, almost hearing the screech of brakes as the car hit him. He fell face forward, his forehead bouncing back from the road like a rubber ball. Then he was beneath the violently braked car. After an instant's shocked horror the crowd on the pavement surged round the car.

The film flickered appreciably, as though the camera operator's hand had been shaking, then stopped.

In the silence of the room the sudden illumination from the chandelier was like the flash of lightning before the peal of thunder.

Ross slowly took his leg from the desk, glancing at Richards, grim-lipped. Richards nodded slightly, then began to wind back the film.

I said incredulously: 'That was Barbara Day driving that car!'

As Ross stubbed out his cigarette he said, quietly: 'Yes. That was Barbara Day.'

'Then that man . . .' I made a vague gesture at the screen. 'The man who was knocked down . . . he must have been . . .'

'Leo Salinger.' Ross turned and faced me. 'That was a film of the accident, Mr. Frazer.'

I half rose from my chair. 'In my camera. But it can't . . .'

From across the projector Richards said calmly: 'Your own film must have been stolen, Frazer. And this one substituted.'

'But how? And when?' I stood up. 'It's impossible. The camera's never been out of my sight. And I haven't been in close enough contact with anyone for them to change the film while I wasn't looking.'

'What about Miss Day?' said Ross smoothly. 'You apparently met her on one or two occasions.'

'Yes, but . . .' I rubbed my left hand desperately across my forehead. 'This doesn't make sense. Even if she had this film, why should she want me to see it?'

Ross made a gesture of impatience. 'For heaven's sake! How should I know why? That's one of the things we've got to find out.' He examined his nails thoughtfully. Then, with disconcerting abruptness, he switched his eyes to mine. 'Did you arrange to see her again?'

'I tried to make a date but she wouldn't play.'

'Any reason why she shouldn't?'

I smiled thinly. 'She does happen to have a fiancé, you know.'

'I think it's time you started giving the fiancé a little competition,' Ross said, matter-of-factly. 'Bump into her once or twice. Casually, of course. I imagine you know the technique.' He gave me a look of faintly amused appraisal. 'But don't play it too hard. If she's up to anything she might get suspicious.'

'I'll do that, sir.' I paused. 'But before I start on' – I risked a grin – 'Assignment Charm, there is one thing I'd like to know about Leo Salinger.'

Ross returned to his desk. 'Go on, Frazer.'

'What was in the parcel he was carrying?'

'In the parcel?' Ross seemed genuinely surprised. 'Why do you ask that?'

I shrugged. 'I'm curious – that's all.'

Ross glanced at me speculatively, then said: 'Salinger was carrying a metronome.'

CHAPTER SIX

I

Back at my flat the telephone bell began ringing the moment I opened the door. Leaving it open, I took the steep stairs two at a time. Not that I was expecting a call. It's just that I'm one of those people who go around biting their fingernails if the phone stops ringing before they've answered it. Kicking open the door of my sitting-room I made a dive for the table and grabbed up the receiver.

'Hello? Tim Frazer speaking,' I panted.

A low, controlled voice said, 'It's Barbara Day. You sound like the finish of the hundred yards dash.'

I laughed. 'Too many cigarettes. It's nice to hear your voice again. How are you, and did you have a good trip back?'

'Yes, it was very pleasant.' The smile went out of her voice as she continued: 'Look, I'm afraid this is very short notice. But I wondered if you'd like to come round for a drink this evening?'

'Of course. I'd love to.'

'My fiancé, Arthur Fairlee, will be here. I know he'd like to meet you.'

'Fine. What time shall I come?'

She hesitated. 'Seven-thirty? Would that be all right?'

'Couldn't be better.'

She laughed lightly. 'How silly of me – you don't know where I live. It's 23 Crawford House Mansions, Chelsea. Can you remember that?'

'I'm scribbling it down.'

'I'll look forward to seeing you then. Good-bye.'

'Good-bye.'

I put down the receiver thoughtfully, wondering why she had telephoned like this out of the blue. Why should she be anxious for me to meet her fiancé? What was the point? Could there be some connection with that strange film of the car accident? I hesitated, wondering if I should telephone Ross. Finally, I decided against it.

2

Crawford House Mansions was one of those modern rabbit warrens in a street off the King's Road. It had a self-operating lift and I took this to the second floor. I went along a carpeted corridor, past half a dozen cell-like doors, until I came to Number 23.

I jabbed a finger at the bell-push, straightened my tie, and conjured up what I hoped was just the right touch of eager expectancy into my smile. I wasted that on a blank door for a couple of minutes, then rang the bell again. As the bell stopped ringing I cocked my head at the door. There was no sound of inner doors being opened or stiletto heels clicking frantically to herald her approach. Just silence.

I glanced at my watch. Three minutes past the half-hour. I frowned at the door. Then I put my thumb on the bell-push and leaned on it.

I took my thumb off the bell after thirty seconds of listening to its mocking ring. I'd phone Barbara Day later, I decided; and if I were feeling half as irritable then as I was now, 'Assignment Charm' wouldn't rate more than a hollow laugh.

I was turning away from the door when I heard a scraping sound at my feet. I looked down. A Yale key was being slipped under the door.

I gaped at it for a moment, then stooped and picked it up. I tossed the key up and down in the palm of my hand, trying to work out the angles. Was this a hint for me to come back later?

Bracing myself, I inserted the key in the lock, opened the door, and entered a small hallway. On the floor, ripped open, was an airline zipper bag. I heeled the door to, then took a closer look at the bag. Attached to the hand grip was a luggage tag. The name on it was M. R. Cordwell.

Opposite me was the half open door of the living room. I crossed to it, pushed it wide, took a step inside, then froze. Lying in the centre of the fitted carpet was a miniature bicycle. Beside it was what had once been a stuffed doll; a Dutchman in national costume. The doll's clothing had been torn open and the stuffing scattered over the carpet. Not far from the doll lay the bulb catalogue, the one Cordwell had produced in Amsterdam. Faintly, my nostrils detected the familiar cigar smoke, and with a chill of apprehension I gazed round the room – at the overturned spindle-legged table, at the gilded lamp beside it, at the shattered china vase and the scattered roses. Then suddenly I noticed the grotesque feet, strangely small for such a big man, pointing at right-angles to each other. I noted the crumpled light-weight suit, the torn lapel, the blood-stained, heavy glass ashtray beside the crew cut, matted hair.

I must have been staring at Cordwell for almost half a minute before becoming aware of the noise. A rhythmic, jubilant ticking that dominated the quiet room. I spun round and made a dive at the metronome lying face upwards on the floor. I stuck my finger against the wagging pendulum. Someone was shouting, 'For God's sake, stop!' It was me. I dropped the instrument back on the floor, straightened up, and went back to Cordwell's body.

I didn't like what I had to do, but there was a chance that the searching of Cordwell's pockets might produce a clue to the identity of his murderer. I stooped down, then jumped back as though I'd been shot. I was as nervous as hell, and the sudden jar of a telephone bell in that room was as unexpected as a shout in a church.

I shook myself like a dog coming out of an ice-cold stream, and turned to the telephone, which was on a small table beside the settee. I hesitated, then went over and picked up the receiver, first covering my hand with my breast-pocket handkerchief.

At once a feminine voice, urgently breathless, came on the line. 'This is Vivien. I was right, Barbara. He's *very* curious about Ericson and Lennard Street. I thought I'd better . . .' The voice wavered uncertainly, then resumed on a more urgent note: 'Barbara, that *is* you, isn't it?'

There was no point in prolonging the call now, so I slid the receiver back onto its cradle, then stood for a moment with my hand still holding it. I tried to get a mental picture of Lennard Street – the name was vaguely familiar – but it eluded me. After a few seconds I replaced my handkerchief and nerved myself to return to the body.

Something told me I hadn't much time, so I began to examine Cordwell's pockets as quickly as possible. There was nothing of any apparent significance in his wallet, and I'd just turned out one of his side pockets when I heard the sound of a latchkey scraping the lock of the front door.

Quickly restoring the odds and ends to his side pocket, I glanced round the room and saw, for the first time, a door in a distant corner. As I crossed over to it I heard the front door open and close. I slipped inside the bedroom, which was obviously Barbara Day's; there was that faint, unmistakable perfume. Leaving the door open a couple of inches I immediately looked round for another exit.

There was only the window, concealed by long silk curtains. I pulled the curtains aside as quietly as possible and breathed a sigh of relief when I saw that it was a French-style window, which was unlatched. Outside was the iron platform of a fire-escape. Leaving the window open, I returned to the door.

I was just in time to see Barbara Day, wearing an attractive summer dress, come through the living room door. She looked puzzled, and I guessed that she'd been surprised to see Cordwell's zipper bag on the hall floor. Her expression changed at the sight of the ravished doll, the overturned chairs, and the bulb catalogue. Then she saw Cordwell's body.

Involuntarily she stepped back a pace, as if to avoid a blow. She was clutching her handbag with both hands, so hard that the whites of her knuckles showed. After what seemed at least a minute she slowly took a cautious step towards the body, then another. There was a tiny click as the toe of her shoe prodded the metronome. She stopped to look at it, her face turned from the body.

The telephone rang and she straightened herself abruptly. I could see a tiny frown wrinkle her forehead; then she suddenly seemed to gain control of herself. She went across and lifted the receiver as if she now welcomed the interruption.

She didn't speak, but listened to the chattering voice, which I could hear faintly though unintelligibly. The corners of her mouth tightened, and at last she interrupted.

'Vivien, get off the line!' she ordered. 'Something dreadful has happened . . .' There was another burst from the earpiece, then Barbara Day lost all patience. 'I must call the police,' she snapped, 'so will you *please* get off the line!'

She slammed down the receiver, her hand trembling slightly as she held it in place to make sure the connection was broken. Then she slowly lifted it again, and I had no difficulty in concluding that she was dialling the familiar 999.

I didn't wait to overhear this conversation, but moved quietly back to the window and out on to the fire-escape.

At the bottom there was a door marked 'Tradesmen'. This led along a stone paved corridor to a push-bar door which opened at a touch, and I found myself in the street. I was faintly surprised to see people strolling casually about their business, the same as any other evening.

A taxi dropped a fare a little way up the street. I hailed it as it came towards me, and said: 'Smith Square.'

As we drove off I looked uneasily through the back window at the entrance to the block of flats, but it seemed quite deserted.

Just as we reached the King's Road a police car swung round the corner almost on two wheels, causing the taxi driver to snatch at his steering wheel.

'Chelsea!' I heard him exclaim. 'Bloody beatniks up to their games again!'

'Live and let live,' I replied, trying to sound as casual as possible, then made no further effort at conversation. It was rather important, I decided, that he should not recall anything about this particular fare.

CHAPTER SEVEN

At Smith Square the door was opened by Hobson, the department's general factotum, a soft-spoken man in a black double-breasted jacket and striped trousers. Mr. Ross, he told me as though revealing a state secret, was not available.

Fuming with frustration I asked if Mr. Richards were available. That got me into the hallway while Hobson went down to the far end of it and whispered confidentially into a house phone. Replacing the receiver silently he told me, in hushed tones, that Mr. Richards could see me.

In the library Richards was sprawled in an easy chair, a whisky and soda in his hand. 'Sorry about Ross. He was called to the House to prime an Under Secretary on a suitably ambiguous answer to . . .' He broke off, eyeing me shrewdly. 'Hello . . . You look as though you'd seen a ghost.'

'The makings of one,' I said. 'Cordwell, the American I saw in Amsterdam, is dead. Murdered.'

Richards whistled silently, then unfolded himself from his chair. 'What you need is a drink.' He crossed to the cocktail cabinet and opened it. 'A brandy I think is indicated.' He examined a bottle. 'Ah, yes. A Courvoisier.' Pouring it, he said, in a conversational tone tactfully intended to bring my nerves off the boil: 'The old boy does himself well in the drink line.

Something of a gourmet, too. You want to time your murders better, Frazer. Say, lunch-time at his club.'

I'd sunk into an easy chair opposite his when he came back with the brandy. 'Sorry to be jumpy,' I said, taking the glass from him. 'But I don't stumble over corpses every day in the week.'

'Unfriendly things,' he said, letting himself down into his chair. 'Ross told me about this American. Like to elaborate, Frazer?'

When I'd outlined the events in Barbara Day's flat Richards pulled at his nose. 'A very unpleasant business. And the murderer left the flat the same way you did – by the fire-escape?'

I nodded. 'After first slipping the latchkey under the front door.'

Richards frowned. 'That's what puzzles me, Frazer. Why make it easy for you to find the body so quickly? You'd think a murderer would want to give himself plenty of time to make his getaway.'

'That had occurred to me.' I sipped my brandy, trying to work it out.

'It could be this way.' Richards closed one eye thought-fully. 'You were expected at the flat. They slipped you the key, knowing damned well you'd go in. Right? Then they tip off the police that a murder's been committed. The police come to the flat, find you there with the body. And . . .'

I cut in on him. 'I *was* expected at the flat. But by Barbara Day.'

Richards eyed me casually over the rim of his glass. 'Well?'

'Oh, come off it, Richards,' I said exasperatedly. 'Barbara Day had nothing to do with the murder. I was watching her from the bedroom as she came into the flat. She was petrified when she saw the body. As for tipping off the police, it was she who telephoned them.'

Richards looked down his nose. 'Witness for the Defence can now leave the box.'

'I'm giving you the facts. Her reactions were those of any woman who finds a dead body in her flat,' I said heatedly. 'Anyway, why would I defend her?'

He gave me an amused glance. 'Our Miss Day's a damned attractive girl,' he reflected. 'I wonder what Cordwell was doing in her flat?'

'I don't know. All I *do* know is that she was as stunned as I was to find him there.'

'You say Cordwell's zipper bag was lying in the hall? And the contents were scattered round his body in the living room?'

'A bulb catalogue, a metronome, and the Dutch doll.'

'That Dutch doll,' Richards said reflectively 'Any theory why the murderer would rip the stuffing out of it?

'An obvious one. He was looking for something that could be hidden in the doll.'

Richards nodded. 'Is there anything special about the metronome?'

'Mechanically it was like any other. But this one was more than usually ornate. Delicately carved and brightly painted, the sort of thing you'd expect to find in the souvenir shops.' My fingers tightened on the stem of my glass. 'Salinger was carrying a metronome when he was accidentally killed, wasn't he? What was that one like?'

'You've just described it pretty accurately.'

'Then . . .' I began.

Richards shook his head. 'This wasn't his. Ross has that locked up in his safe. I managed to get possession of it after the inquest.' He smiled. 'This department does manage to pull a string or two sometimes, you know, Frazer.'

I looked suitably impressed, then finished my brandy. 'Well, where do we go from here?'

'So far as you're concerned – nowhere, for the moment.' He got up, and took my glass and his over to the cocktail cabinet. 'The police will be at Miss Day's flat now, questioning her. If she's as genuine as you think she is, she'll tell them she was expecting you tonight.'

'I'd take a bet on that,' I said sharply. 'And there's no need to be sarcastic about it.'

'Did I sound sarcastic?' he said smoothly. 'The point I was making was this. You'll need to think up a pretty plausible story to keep the police off your toes.'

'I'll just tell them the truth. I've nothing to hide.'

'Haven't you?' Richards handed me another Courvoisier, then took his own glass for a walk up and down the room. 'You found the body. Why didn't you wait until they came to the flat and tell them about it? The police won't like that at all.' He waved his glass at me, restrainingly. 'Oh, *we* know why you came dashing round here to report to Ross. But the police won't say, "Thanks very much, Mr. Frazer, that lets you out!" when you tell them you were doing a tail job on Barbara Day. They'll be very curious indeed.'

'Well, suppose they are?' I said, shrugging. 'All I have to do is mention this department . . .'

'That's just what you haven't got to do,' Richards said quickly, swinging round on me. 'Get this into your head, Frazer. All Ross is concerned with is why one of his most trusted agents should have been killed. That we disagree as to it being an accident is beside the point. Your assignment is to find out whether Miss Day is mixed up with people who wanted Salinger out of the way. And to do that she mustn't know you're tailing her. Tell the police you are, and they'll make big feet noises that will divert her shell-like ears in *your* direction. And not quite so charmingly as they are at present.'

'It's back-handed, but I'll take it as a compliment on my handling of the assignment so far,' I said, grinning up at him. 'By the way, do you still think it was an accident?'

'This American being murdered in her flat certainly opens up possibilities.' He pursed his lips thoughtfully, then said decisively: 'Phone her now. Give her some reason why you didn't turn up.' He went over to the desk and flicked through the pages of a diary on it. 'Here we are . . . Her number's Chelsea 7146. Use the green telephone. It's an outside line.'

I crossed to the desk, picked up the receiver, and dialled the number slowly, figuring out a plausible excuse.

I put the receiver to my ear and heard the ringing tone. A couple of seconds later there was a click as the receiver was lifted at the other end.

A man's voice came crisply on the line. 'Chelsea 7146.'

I hesitated, then after a slightly surprised, 'Oh – er . . .' I went on briskly: 'Could I speak to Miss Day? My name's Frazer.'

There was the unmistakable hand-blanketing of the mouth-piece at the other end, and I lip-spoke 'Police' to Richards. He smiled back sagely. Then I was listening to Barbara Day's voice. 'Is that you, Mr. Frazer?'

'I say, I'm terribly sorry about tonight,' I said with, I hoped, an authentic note of frantic apology in my voice. 'But I had a business appointment at Slough. I forgot all about it when I accepted your invitation. I was hoping to get back in time, but this conference went on and on. As a matter of fact, I'm speaking from Slough at the moment.'

'Bad luck. I mean about your conference. I wondered what had happened to you.'

'I did ring before I left but couldn't get a reply.' I glanced across at Richards who seemed amused. 'It was about a quarter past seven.'

'Oh, did you? I wasn't in then. Arthur, my fiancé, rang me earlier. He had one of his asthma attacks and I thought I ought to go round and make sure he was all right.' A smile came into her voice. 'If you had come you'd have been ringing the bell of an empty flat. Still, some other time, perhaps.'

I said I hoped so, apologised again, and hung up.

'Nice work,' Richards said, taking a cigarette from the silver box and pushing it across to me. 'Where was she at a quarter past seven?'

'Apparently her fiancé was ill and she went round to look after him.'

'You can rely on the police to check that,' Richards said, with a sardonic glance at me. 'You want to watch out, Frazer. They'll be looking for a motive for Cordwell's murder. Something nice and primitive, like jealousy, for instance.'

CHAPTER EIGHT

It was just after eight when I awoke next morning. I could hear Mrs. Glover, my daily woman, rattling cups in the kitchen. An aroma of coffee drifted in as I reached for a cigarette from the case on the bedside table. I had a lot of mental sorting-out to do and I've a Churchillian habit of doing most of my constructive thinking in bed.

A report of the murder should be in the morning paper and I decided to see whether there were any fresh developments. As I was about to call to Mrs. Glover to bring the newspaper and coffee to me in bed, the front door bell rang.

Mrs. Glover bustled past, slightly breathless as usual. Then she was back, knocking on my door. 'A gentleman to see you, sir.'

Usually I'm 'Mr Frazer' to her, unless she wants to impress my visitors. Latterly, these had been creditors connected with my defunct business; only my name on a cheque would have impressed *them*.

Cursing, I groped for my slippers and dragged on my blue dressing-gown, pausing only to comb my hair and slip the cigarette case into my pocket.

Mrs. Glover was lurking outside my door, a look of concern on her usually cheerful face. 'It's a plain-clothes man,' she hissed. 'I can smell 'em!'

This was it. Thrusting my hands in my dressing-gown pockets I strolled casually into the living room.

A tall man, with neatly brushed hair greying at the sides, wearing a dark suit and grey tie, watched my entrance with a slightly quizzical look, plainly alert for anything that might be construed as suspicious.

'Mr. Frazer?' he began affably. 'My name's Trueman – Detective-Inspector Trueman.'

I frowned perplexedly. 'What's the trouble, Inspector? Another complaint about my parking in front of my next door neighbour's garage?'

'Nothing as heinous as that, sir,' he said, with a policeman's heavy humour. 'It's about a lady I believe you know, Mr. Frazer. A Miss Barbara Day.'

'Yes, she's a friend of mine.' I looked startled. 'Nothing's happened to her, has it? An accident?'

He shook his head. 'I'd just like to ask you a few questions about her.' His grey eyes had been casually roaming the room; suddenly they came up to mine. 'You had an appointment with her yesterday evening?' It was more a statement than a question.

'That's right,' I said in a puzzled manner. 'At seven-thirty, at her flat. Unfortunately I was unable to keep the appointment. I was held up at Slough.'

'I see,' he said in a non-committal tone. 'Then you weren't at Crawford House Mansions at any time yesterday evening?'

'I've already told you that, Inspector,' I replied irritably.

'You've told me you weren't there at seven-thirty,' he corrected.

'Let's get this clear, Inspector. So far as I know, I've never been within half a mile of – whatever the mansions are called.' His smooth smile provoked me into asking: 'Why this third degree stuff?'

He didn't like that at all. For an instant it got him on the wrong foot. 'I'm sorry you take it that way, sir.' He fidgeted with his stiff-brimmed, dark grey hat. 'This is purely routine questioning.' Then his tone sharpened. 'A man was murdered last night – in Miss Day's flat.'

I did my best to look startled again, then asked: 'Have you found the murderer?'

'No.' He paused. 'I understand you knew the murdered man.'

'*I* did!'

'His name's Cordwell.'

'Cordwell . . . Cordwell,' I said, frowning. Then I snapped my fingers. 'Of course! He was the man I met with Miss Day in Amsterdam. Although I can scarcely say I knew him – I only saw him that once.'

'Miss Day told me about the incident.' He smiled obliquely as though he'd very nearly trapped me. 'Would you say Miss Day was on friendly terms with him?'

I shrugged. 'No more than the casual friendship of people who meet each other abroad on holiday.'

He watched his finger run round the braided brim of his hat. 'And you were all meeting again in her flat last night to talk over your holiday in Amsterdam?'

I fished out my cigarette case to gain time while I tried to find the barb in the question. 'She didn't tell me Cordwell was coming,' I said, offering him my case. 'As a matter of fact,

I thought he'd gone back to America. I was invited to meet her fiancé.'

'That's what she said.' He took a cigarette from my case. 'Miss Day's a very attractive woman, wouldn't you say, Mr. Frazer?'

I smiled, remembering Richards' motive-theory. 'Blondes are my weakness,' I said.

As I snapped my lighter to his cigarette Trueman glanced up at me. 'Does Miss Day's fiancé know that you are an eligible young bachelor?'

'As it happens,' I said tartly, 'I wouldn't have met Miss Day's fiancé. It seems he was taken ill yesterday evening.' I smiled tauntingly. 'Tell me if I'm wrong, Inspector, but I think you were in her flat when she told me.'

'Quite right. I was,' he said imperturbably, glancing at his watch. 'Thanks for your help, Mr. Frazer. Don't bother to come to the front door.' He made a gesture of good-bye with his hat as he went out of the living room, then he turned back to me. 'We checked on the asthma attack. Miss Day was with her fiancé from six-thirty to well after seven. We like to confirm alibis, Mr. Frazer.'

When he'd gone Mrs. Glover came in with a tray of coffee and toast. 'Was it about your car, Mr. Frazer?' she asked innocently. 'That man next door was swearing something dreadful yesterday when it was parked outside his garage door.'

'Odd you should think that, Mrs. Glover,' I said, grinning at her. 'They were almost the exact words I used when I saw the detective.'

Producing a newspaper from under the tray she placed it on the table. 'There's been another murder in Chelsea, Mr. Frazer,' she said, unnecessarily rearranging the contents of the tray.

'So the detective was telling me,' I said.

She seemed to get the implication, and bustled out indignantly.

I poured myself a coffee, lit a cigarette, and picked up the paper. It was conveniently folded to display the Stop Press. I skimmed it quickly. It merely said that a man had been found in a Chelsea luxury flat, and that the tenant, Miss Barbara Day, was helping the police in their inquiries.

I put the paper down and went back over my talk with Trueman. One thing stuck out a mile – Barbara Day hadn't withheld anything from him. That confirmed my views on her. She knew no more about Cordwell's murder than I did.

But what was the American doing in her flat? And how did he get in? I was pouring myself another cup of coffee when I recollected something that Trueman had said. 'You were all meeting again in her flat last night to talk over your holiday in Amsterdam?' Coffee was pouring over the top of the cup into the saucer before I realised what I was doing. With a muttered 'Damn' I replaced the percolator on the table, got up, crossed over to the telephone and dialled Chelsea 7146.

I listened to the engaged signal for half a minute, then replaced the receiver and came back to the table. I lit another cigarette from the stub of the last, dropped that into the coffee-filled saucer, and tossed the inference of Trueman's words around in my mind. Was that the excuse Barbara Day had used to get Cordwell round to her flat? To meet me and talk over our holiday? But why? To murder him? I saw again the body and the battered head, with the heavy, blood-stained glass ashtray beside it. It simply did not add up. Cordwell was a powerful man; a blow from one of his heavy fists would have knocked any woman senseless. Besides, I had seen Barbara Day when she came into the flat. There was nothing in her appearance to suggest she'd been in a fight. But someone must have let Cordwell into the flat. And who-ever did so was the person who slipped the key under the door to me. Circumstantially, that person was the murderer; but not necessarily.

A dozen conjectures later I gave up. I was in the bath when it suddenly occurred to me that Trueman hadn't urged me to disclose where I'd been the previous evening. It would have been awkward if he'd pressed me to detail my movements. Why hadn't he done so, I wondered? I had an uncomfortable feeling that he suspected I'd kept the appointment with Barbara Day, and was just keeping me on the end of a line until he was ready to haul me in like a floundering fish.

When I was dressed I tried again to contact Miss Day. At ten o'clock, after a third abortive attempt, I decided that an engaged line meant she was in her flat, and that I'd go round there.

I called to Mrs. Glover that I was leaving, then went down to the mews and got my Jaguar out of the garage under my flat. From behind my living room curtain a face watched me go. I flicked a derisive hand towards the garage next door. Mrs. Glover knew damn well I never parked my car outside it.

CHAPTER NINE

Pressing the bell of the flat at Crawford House Mansions reminded me it was little more than twelve hours since I'd been standing there expectantly. Involuntarily, my glance dropped to the bottom of the door. I'd almost expected to see a key pushed slowly under it, and it came as a shock when the door was suddenly flung wide.

'Tim! . . . Mr. Frazer . . .'

I couldn't help noticing the relief in her voice.

'I hope I haven't dropped in at an awkward time,' I said, noting the fur coat draped over her shoulders. 'But I tried to ring you . . .'

She made a gesture, half welcoming, half apologetic. 'Oh, I'm sorry. If I'd known . . . but I've had my receiver off all morning. Those reporters were driving me crazy!' She bit her lip. 'Then this detective and his endless questions . . .'

I interrupted her quickly. 'I've just had a visit from Inspector Trueman.'

'I was afraid you would,' she said contritely. 'I had to tell him about you when you phoned. But please come in, Mr. Frazer.'

I followed her into the now tidy living room. 'My friends call me Tim,' I said with a smile.

She made a little face at me. 'It slipped out.' She motioned me to a chintz-covered easy chair. 'Do sit down, Tim.'

Slipping out of the fur coat, she let it fall on to the settee. She wore a red suit, ornamented by a single diamond-encrusted lovers'-knot brooch. 'Forgive me if I'm rather remote,' she said taking the easy chair opposite mine and crossing her legs negligently, 'but I haven't yet really recovered from the shock. You read about such things in the papers; you can't believe it can happen to you.'

I nodded sympathetically. 'When the detective told me, I was appalled.' I got out my cigarette case and opened it slowly. 'What I couldn't grasp was that it should be Cordwell. I thought he'd gone back to the States days ago.' I raised my eyes from the case, watching her face.

Her forehead furrowed. 'It's beyond me. I was under the impression he flew back from Amsterdam the day after we met him at *De Kroon*.' She shrugged helplessly. 'I didn't see him again after that.'

I held out my cigarette case. 'He didn't mention that he might look you up some time if he did come over here?'

'Never even hinted at it.' She took a cigarette, and I put a light to it. 'That detective kept trying to make me admit we'd arranged to meet here.'

'He did the same thing to me. I think he was a bit disappointed when I told him you hardly knew the man.'

She smiled gratefully. 'I'm terribly sorry to have involved you in all this. But what could I do? I had to tell him I was expecting you at seven-thirty.'

'That's all right.' I held my lighter hesitantly to my own cigarette. 'If you were going out don't let me upset any arrangements.'

Her eyes smiled into mine. 'It's thoughtful of you. But it really wasn't all that urgent. I'd been expecting Arthur to call round; he usually does on his way to his office. Of all mornings he had to miss this one – just when I needed his shoulder to cry on.' Her fingers tapped at the arm of her chair. 'So I was about to descend on him in person. But perhaps I shouldn't be too furious with him. He must be feeling pretty rotten after that attack of asthma yesterday evening.'

'Of course, that's why you were out when I rang the first time – at seven-fifteen.'

'Yes.' She looked at the toe of her shoe. 'You were phoning from . . . Slough, wasn't it?'

'That's right.'

'For your technical magazine, or whatever it was?' Her voice wavered uncertainly. 'You *did* say you were a journalist, didn't you?'

If Trueman began digging into my past, I thought, he'd soon come up with the true facts. 'I do write for the engineering magazines at times,' I said truthfully. 'You see, I'm actually an engineer. I had my own works until recently. Unfortunately it went broke.'

'Oh, bad luck,' she commiserated. 'Then you were at Slough . . . ?' She left the question dangling inescapably.

It was then that I had a brain-wave. By making my visit to Slough sufficiently obscure I'd forestall any too direct inquiries that Trueman might make about its object. 'I didn't want to have to tell you this, Barbara. But I went down there on the off-chance of getting myself fixed up with one of the engineering firms.' I laughed awkwardly. 'I just wandered about, looking them over and trying to force myself to call on one, cap in hand. In the end I dithered around until I'd messed up our appointment.'

'As though *that* mattered.' Her face clouded. 'But it did, didn't it? If you had come at half-past seven poor Mr. Cordwell . . .'

I broke the momentary silence. 'How did he get into your flat, Barbara? Why was he here?'

'Please,' she begged. 'I went through all this for *hours* last night with the detective.'

'I had the impression he wasn't entirely convinced Cordwell was no more than a casual acquaintance of yours.' At that moment it seemed important to force a direct answer out of her. 'Was that all he was, Barbara?'

'I'd never seen the man until I met him at the hotel,' she replied angrily. Then, with a shrug, she said wearily: 'I suppose I'd better tell you. I was lying when I said I never saw him again after our meeting at *De Kroon*.' She avoided my eyes, then said in a low voice: 'He came to my room that night.'

'And . . . ?'

'He made a pass at me.' She spread her hands. 'Nothing happened. He calmed down eventually and apologised. Some nonsense about having fallen for me from the moment he saw me at London Airport.'

'Did you tell the Inspector this?' When she shook her head I asked: 'Why not?'

'And have him tell Arthur?' she demanded quickly.

'What if he did?' I smiled. 'Fairlee surely doesn't imagine an engagement ring puts a barbed wire fence round an attractive girl?'

'I'm afraid he does. Perhaps its his asthma that makes him so intolerant.' Her eyes met mine for a long moment. 'It's absurd, but I think he's even jealous of you.'

The door bell pealed stridently.

I laughed briefly. 'Of me!'

Then the bell rang again, a prolonged, insistent ring.

She stood up. 'It sounds as though you and Arthur may be meeting after all.'

As she went out to admit her visitor I stubbed out my cigarette in an ashtray emblazoned with the arms of Amsterdam.

A high-pitched voice drifted in from the hallway. 'What's happened, Barbara? Why didn't you ring me?' There was some heavy breathing. 'A police Inspector just called round and said . . .'

Barbara's voice interrupted quietly. 'Please, Arthur – don't get so excited. Your asthma . . .'

'Don't get excited!' The voice rose to a crescendo. 'Good God, Barbara . . . don't you realise . . .'

'Oh, do please calm down, Arthur,' Barbara said sharply. 'Mr. Frazer's in there.'

'Frazer?' Fairlee's voice was explosive with suspicion. 'Frazer? The man you met on the plane?'

I didn't catch her admonitory whisper.

A moment later I was standing up, murmuring, 'How do

you do?' to a tall, desiccated man with dark hair parted in the centre, a cropped moustache, beak-like nose, and pale-blue eyes that stared at me hostilely through heavy hornrims. He was taking off his bowler as he came in; the impeccably rolled umbrella completed the picture.

'Mr. Frazer,' Barbara said, 'this is my fiancé, Arthur Fairlee.'

He hung a limp hand at me. 'Barbara has mentioned you,' he said coldly, and withdrew his hand from mine as though it held a soiled handkerchief. He turned to Barbara. 'I want to talk to you, Barbara. Alone, if you don't mind.'

'It's all right, darling,' she said soothingly. 'Mr. Frazer knows what happened. That's why he's here.'

'I thought there might be something I could do to help,' I said quickly. 'It's a pretty awful business.'

'Pretty awful. My God, that's an understatement, if you like!' With an effort Fairlee recovered his breath after this outburst. 'Who is this man Cordwell? I demand an explanation, Barbara! You've never mentioned him to me before.'

'He wasn't that important,' she said, with a glance of mock despair at me. 'Just a casual acquaintance we met in Amsterdam.'

Fairlee pointed his umbrella at me accusingly. 'You've met this Cordwell?'

'On one occasion. I was with Miss Day. We met him over some drinks.'

'Drinks? We?' he panted, glancing from one to the other suspiciously. 'How did this fellow Cordwell come to be here? I'm not a fool, Barbara. There must be a lot more to this than appears on the surface.'

I wondered how the devil Barbara came to be engaged to this querulous neurotic. In a mildly sarcastic tone, I said: 'You've got something there, Mr. Fairlee.'

He glared at me. 'I wasn't talking to you, sir.'

Barbara sighed. 'Oh, Arthur, please.'

'Get a grip on yourself, Fairlee,' I said roughly. 'Miss Day's had a very unpleasant experience. Right now she needs sympathy, not bullying.'

His lips tightened angrily for a moment, then he smiled bleakly. 'How right you are. I apologise, Frazer.' He turned to Barbara. 'I'm sorry, dear. I think we should postpone any further discussion until I'm less upset. This evening, then.' He glanced at his watch. 'T'ck, t'ck! I'm due at a Board meeting in half an hour. By the way, Barbara, do something about that partner of yours. She's phoned me three times to say she can't get hold of you.'

'Of course I will, darling,' Barbara said placatingly. 'I expect Vivien's furious with me because I hung up on her last night.' She shuddered. 'It was just at the moment when I'd seen the . . .'

Fairlee's eyes followed the direction of hers. He was about to say something when the door bell interrupted him.

Barbara gave another little sigh. 'Why can't they leave me in peace?'

'If it's the newspapers don't tell them anything!' Fairlee ordered sharply. 'Not a word now, Barbara! My name mustn't be mentioned; you understand?'

'Don't worry, darling. I think I can handle them.' She crossed the room, patting his arm reassuringly as she passed.

Fairlee tapped his thigh irritably with his bowler. 'Publicity of this sort would play the devil with my business.' He glared at me as though I were responsible for the situation. 'I'm a stockbroker, Frazer.'

'I think you can trust Miss Day to deal with reporters tactfully,' I said. I took out my cigarette case, proffering it to him. He shook his head, patting his chest in explanation. 'Miss Day mentioned that she had an antique business,' I said when I'd lit a cigarette. 'You say she has a partner – Vivien . . . ?'

'Yes, yes,' he replied testily. 'Vivien Gilmore and my fiancée are in partnership.' He glanced round impatiently, eager to be gone.

From the door Barbara said: 'It's Inspector Trueman, darling.'

I turned. Trueman stood in the doorway, his eyes roaming the room as though making an inventory of everything in it. When they met mine he nodded. 'Good morning, sir.'

Turning his back on Trueman, Fairlee said: 'I'm late now, Barbara. I must go.' He waggled his umbrella at me. 'Can I give you a lift?'

Trueman stepped forward. 'I'd like a word with Mr. Frazer, if you don't mind, sir.'

Fairlee gave me a long, speculative look, then nodded curtly and walked past Trueman to the door.

'Excuse me, Inspector,' Barbara said brightly, and followed Fairlee from the room.

CHAPTER TEN

I

'Cosy flat, isn't it, sir?'

I'd been following Barbara with my eyes, and I now turned to find Trueman watching me, a slight smile on his thin lips. 'Very,' I said tersely.

'First time you've been here, isn't it, sir?'

With some effort I replied unemotionally: 'I made it quite plain this morning that I'd never been invited here until last night.'

He raised one eyebrow quizzically. 'And you couldn't keep that appointment, could you, Mr. Frazer?'

Before I could answer, Barbara came back. She closed the door carefully, then turned to us. 'Oh, please, do sit down both of you.'

Trueman took a hard-backed chair, facing the two Barbara and I had occupied a few minutes before. 'Miss Day,' he said, resting his hat on his knees, 'does the name Ericson mean anything to you?'

I inhaled cigarette smoke, waiting for her reaction. But it was no more than you'd expect from somebody suddenly confronted with a name completely strange to them.

'No,' she said blankly. 'I'm afraid it doesn't.'

Trueman glanced at me. 'And you, sir?'

I shook my head. 'It doesn't ring a bell with me, either. Should it?'

'Not if Cordwell was just a casual acquaintance,' he told us. 'It would have been helpful in our efforts to check Cordwell's background if you had known the name. It was written in a diary we found on his body. Apparently he had appointments with this Ericson for today, tomorrow, and the day after.' Trueman's tone sharpened. 'Miss Day . . . I'd like you to tell me again how many times you met Cordwell in Amsterdam.'

'Oh, *really*!' she said with exasperation. 'I've already told you – the only occasion was when we were with Mr. Frazer at *De Kroon*.'

Trueman drew the edge of his hand along the dent of his hat. 'Would you like to think that over, Miss Day, and answer the question again?'

She retorted, rather too dramatically: 'Are you accusing me of lying, Inspector?'

He gave a little shrug, then after a moment said calmly: 'We have definite proof that you met him on another occasion, Miss Day.'

I stiffened as she queried in a more uncertain tone: 'What sort of proof, Inspector?'

He leaned forward. 'A movie film, Miss Day. A movie film that we found on the dead man. I ran it through an hour ago. There are some shots of Amsterdam – with yourself in several of them. One in particular is of the *Café De Kroon*. It shows Cordwell joining you at a table.' He cleared his throat.

'You appeared to be more than a casual acquaintance, if I may say so.'

I suppose I must have betrayed some reaction to hearing that my film had been found in Cordwell's possession. The Inspector's slightly malicious smile suggested that he'd put a different interpretation on my expression. 'You don't appear to have been present on that occasion, Mr. Frazer.'

'It may surprise you to know, Inspector,' I said unpleasantly, 'that the film was taken by me.'

For once his urbanity deserted him. 'You took it, sir?'

Barbara sat up, her eyes shining. 'Tim! but of course you took it! I remember it now.'

'Just a minute,' Trueman said, the sceptical expression on his face once again. 'If you took that film, sir, what was it doing in Cordwell's pocket?'

I thought I knew the answer, but didn't want to get involved with Trueman over the film. 'That's your pigeon, Inspector,' I said. 'I lost that film somewhere along the line – probably in Amsterdam.'

Trueman frowned at this unexpected development, then said quietly. 'Let me know if anything more definite occurs to you. You can always leave a message for me at the Yard.' He stood up. 'Well, that's all for the moment, I think. By the way, Miss Day, you're not planning to go to Amsterdam again in the near future?'

'Heavens, no!' she exclaimed. 'What put that thought in your head?'

'I just wanted to be sure you'd still be here if I wanted you.'

He stood looking down at her, then with an, 'I'll see myself out,' left so abruptly that we were both a little surprised.

As the front door closed Barbara gave a sigh of relief. 'Thank goodness he's gone!' She smiled. 'I didn't know you were taking pictures of me all over Amsterdam, Tim.'

'I saw you once or twice,' I said, off-handedly. 'I thought I'd like to include an attractive girl on my Dutch backgrounds.'

'That's sweet of you,' she said warmly. 'Where did you see me?'

'Oh . . . coming out of museums . . . on bridges . . . getting off boats,' I replied rather lamely.

She smiled again. 'I remember that one,' she said softly.

I rose. 'I must be getting along now,' I said, feeling vaguely ill at ease.

'It's been nice having you here to give me your moral support,' she said gratefully. 'How like Arthur to walk out on me just when I need him.'

At the front door I said, 'You will let me know if there's any development, Barbara?'

'Of course.' She looked up into my face. 'You'll be the first to know, Tim.'

2

I stopped at the first call-box, to telephone Richards.

After the preliminary greetings he asked suavely: 'Any news of the bewitching Barbara?'

'You remember I mentioned that a phone call came through for her whilst I was in the flat last night, and I answered it?'

'It did crop up among the lurid details. You didn't get around to telling me what was said.'

'By me, nothing,' I said, a trifle nettled by his bantering tone. 'It was from a woman who announced herself as Vivien. She went right on talking. So far as I can remember, she said, "I was right, Barbara. He's *very* curious about Ericson . . ."'

Richards cut in. 'What was that name again?'

'Ericson.' My hand tightened on the receiver. 'Why did you ask me to repeat it?'

'I just didn't catch it at first,' he said casually. 'Well, go on . . .'

'Well, Vivien turns out to be a Miss Gilmore – Barbara Day's partner in the antique shop.'

'Have you been to the shop, then?'

'No, I went round to Barbara's – Miss Day's flat this morning. Her fiancé was there and he let the information out more or less incidentally.'

'So he's turned up!' Richards laughed. 'What's he like?'

'Rather like you, as a matter of fact, Richards. An absolute bastard!'

I let him say his piece, then went on: 'While I was at Miss Day's flat a detective – Inspector Trueman – arrived. He'd already given me a grilling earlier this morning. He said he'd taken a diary from Cordwell's pocket, which recorded several appointments with this man Ericson. Trueman threw the name at Miss Day; she said it didn't mean a thing to her.'

'H'm . . .' Richards paused. 'You think she was lying?'

'I'm damned sure she was,' I said acidly. 'When Vivien Gilmore phoned she obviously took it for granted that Miss Day knew Ericson – and the street name, too.'

'Street name? You didn't mention a street name before!' Richards said sharply.

'For the simple reason that I've forgotten the name of it,' I said, frowning at myself in the call-box mirror. 'Lennox Street . . . Lenley . . . Lenton . . . It's right on the tip of my tongue . . .'

'Let me give *you* a tip, Frazer. Always get a name down directly you hear it. On the back of an envelope – anywhere, but get it down.' Then he laughed apologetically. 'Sorry to sound off like a Sergeant-Major, but one of the first things you have to learn is never to rely on your memory. I'll see if we have an Ericson in our records. Don't forget to ring me if you remember that street name.'

There was a decent-looking pub a step or two from the callbox, so I parked my car there and treated myself to a cheese roll and a tankard of bitter. Then I drove back to my flat, edging through a couple of yellows, more intent on recalling the street name than on my driving.

CHAPTER ELEVEN

I took my key from the front door and was about to stub out my cigarette in the ashtray on the hall table when I heard a faint rustling of paper coming from my living room. Then a drawer was jerked open. I knew it wasn't Mrs. Glover; she always left promptly at twelve.

Leaving the front door ajar I stepped across the hallway and peered through the crack of the half open living room door. I could just see a hand foraging amongst the papers in my writing bureau.

I eased the door open a little further. A man in a well cut grey suit stood with his back towards me. The slim waist and powerful sloping shoulders warned me I'd need every one of the ten years' difference in our ages if it came to a showdown.

I took a step inside the room and said quietly: 'You won't find any money there, if that's what you're looking for.'

He spun round and we faced one another in silence, each sizing up the other. His eyes were dark in a sallow face. Above a hard mouth was a pencil-line moustache. He was a type that you see in West End bars, reading the racing results in the Stop Press and shiftily avoiding the eyes of any stranger.

He refused to meet my eyes now as I challenged him. 'Who are you, anyway?'

He smiled tightly. 'I'll bounce that one back at you, Frazer. Who the hell are *you*?'

'You seem to know my name, anyway,' I said, stepping towards a side table and reaching for the telephone. 'Maybe you prefer the police to ask the questions?'

'Keep your hands off that phone, Frazer!'

My hand retreated as though it had been stung. I was looking down the muzzle of a .38 automatic.

'What's the game?' he asked. 'Why are you trailing Barbara Day?'

'Trailing her?' I said. 'She's a friend of mine.'

'She wasn't until you met her on the plane to Amsterdam.'

'Where did you get that information?'

'We got it!' he snapped. 'Now we want some information about you, Frazer.'

I'd been doing some quick thinking while this exchange was going on. My living room has a parquet floor, with mats placed here and there. This was the day that Mrs. Glover waxed the floor, and no rose had ever smelled so sweet as did the pungent odour of the wax at that moment.

'You're holding the cards,' I said, nodding towards the gun. 'But why not short circuit the story of my life and come to the point?' I looked at the end of my cigarette. His eyes followed mine and I took a step forward. 'What is it you really want to know?'

'Don't play the innocent,' he said roughly. 'What have you done with them?'

'Done with them?' There was no need for me to fake my surprise.

He waved the gun impatiently. 'You want me to spell it?'

He was standing on a small rug near the desk. 'Oh, well . . . I suppose I'd better . . .' I began – then, 'Damn!' I exclaimed and dropped the cigarette to the floor. 'Burnt my fingers talking to . . .' I stopped quickly and grabbed at the edge of the rug. It was thin and slid across the waxed floor as though it were ice. The man fell backwards, the gun falling from his hand and slithering across the floor to the wall.

I made a dive for it, but he rolled over, clutched one of my ankles, and jerked me forward on to the floor. The next instant he was on top of me. I'd been right about the power in the sloping shoulders.

The wax didn't smell quite so sweet now that my nose was flattened against it. I got my left leg round one of his, pressed the palm of my right hand on to the floor, and rolled him over. Raising my head, I looked for the gun; it was six inches from my left hand. I reached out for it . . . then something cracked in my head and I was falling down into the pitch darkness of an abyss . . .

The dull, rhythmic pain of a pendulum inside my head woke me. I felt old and tired. At the top of the abyss there were voices and light . . . I clawed my way up to them . . . Then the smell of wax seemed to restore my full consciousness.

The voice of the man I'd been struggling with was saying: 'No, they weren't in the bureau.'

'Nor on him,' said another voice – a cultured voice, which chose words with the preciseness of someone speaking a language not their own. 'I would not have done this, Lloyd; but in another moment he would have had the gun.' My assailant laughed shortly. 'He's tougher than he looks.'

'I hope so,' the other voice remarked gravely. 'The bedroom, Lloyd? You had better look round in there.'

The door closed. Then I felt a hand in my inside pocket, removing my cigarette case. I lay motionless until I heard the sound of the cigarette case being put down on the bureau, then turned my head round enough to get a one-eyed look at this man. He had his back to me and appeared to be writing. He was shorter and younger than the man I had caught rifling my bureau. His fair hair was close-cropped at the back and sides. I had the impression of a man who took a pride in his appearance. Then my cigarette case was snapped shut and I closed my eyes as he turned back to me.

He'd just replaced the cigarette case in my pocket when the man called Lloyd returned.

'Nothing there.'

'I have a feeling you were mistaken, Lloyd. I do not think that Frazer is connected with those others.' From the direction of his voice I guessed that he was standing over me.

'I'm beginning to have some doubts myself . . .' Lloyd broke off, with an abrupt: 'Anyway, we shall have to see what happens from now on. Let's move, before he comes round.'

I waited until I heard the front door close, then rolled over and sat up. My head throbbed worse than ever, and I put a hand gingerly to the back of it. There was a lump as big as an egg, but no blood on my hand when I took it away.

With an effort I levered myself up and staggered across to the drinks table. I poured myself four fingers of whisky and gulped it down; then I stood looking down at the empty glass while the whisky gradually began to take effect, and presently I took out my cigarette case. Tucked under the cigarettes was a slip of paper. I drew it out and read the scrawled message. Just two words.

LENNARD STREET

'Lennard Street,' I muttered. 'By God, that was it! Lennard Street!'

I was still shaky as the devil and not thinking too coherently, so I decided to take a shower. Afterwards I stretched out on the settee and thought over what had happened since I'd come into my flat.

From what the man Lloyd had said to me it was obvious that I was suspected of having something. His 'What have you done with them?' could imply anything from plans to banknotes. Whatever the 'something' was he was prepared to use a gun to get it. But where did Barbara Day fit into all this? And why did he want to know my reason for trailing her?

Suddenly I remembered the Dutch doll, ripped open and lying by the body. Had Cordwell been carrying the 'something' in that? I wondered for a moment whether I'd been face to face with Cordwell's murderer an hour before. But I dismissed the thought; his assailant would have found what he was after in the doll. The two intruders were obviously under the impression that I had killed and robbed Cordwell.

From the glimpse I'd had of him and the snatches of over-heard conversation, I'd got the idea that the second man was the more intelligent of the two. That he was uncertain about me was obvious in everything he had said. But why insert the note in my cigarette case?

I fingered the lump on the back of my head tenderly. I didn't think I'd been struck with the butt of the gun. The skin was unbroken. I hadn't noticed any sign of my front door having been forced when I'd come in; that indicated that they'd used the old thieves' trick of slipping a piece of celluloid into the door latch. But the second man, at least, didn't look or talk like a thug.

Tomorrow, after a good night's sleep, I would do some prowling round Lennard Street. But I wouldn't tell Richards until I'd first had a good look round for myself.

CHAPTER TWELVE

I found it among the maze of streets in the area south of Hyde Park, bounded by Sloane Street on the east and Exhibition Road on the west. It was a fairly busy street, used by traffic cutting through to Brompton Road.

Parking my car down a side turning I walked back to Lennard Street. Its shops catered for what in another age would have been called the carriage trade. There were several dress and hat shops, prices not shown, a jeweller's, a hand-made-pottery shop, a health-food store, a picture framer's, and so on. It seemed the least likely street for a man with an egg-sized bump on his head to be wandering down in search of . . . Well, in search of what? I asked myself, gazing vacantly into the window of an espresso bar.

Breaking from a reverie I suddenly realised that I was staring at a quaint Dutch doll – a little man riding a toy bicycle. My eyes wandered to the other objects in the window – a pair of wooden clogs, some fibre-filled bowls with tulips flowering in them, a model of a windmill. I looked up at the name running in gold script across the window. *The Dyke*, it said. I thought a coffee in there might help to set my brain working.

It was the usual sort of espresso bar. The coffee machine, looking like a miniature juke-box, was in the centre of a long counter. In front of this were a dozen bar stools. To the right were tables and chairs for those who preferred to put their heads together. The Dutch motif of the window was even more prominent inside. Tourist publicity posters of Holland in tulip time decorated the walls, interspersed with hanging clogs. Pots of tulips were on every table. At the nearest end of the counter was a six-foot flat cut-out of a windmill. I went in behind it and perched myself on a stool.

In the mirror behind the counter I had a full view of the tables. The sole occupant of these, just visible between the sails of the windmill, was a blonde wearing a close-fitting emerald green dress.

A harassed girl, dressed in a tulip-patterned smock, string-like hair hanging down to her shoulders, swept a used coffee cup and saucer from the counter in front of me. 'Yes, sir?' she said, adenoidally disinterested.

I ordered a coffee and idly watched her manipulate the chromium monster. As she came back with my couple of inches of coffee beneath its coronet of froth the woman behind me called: 'My bill, please, Carol.'

The waitress searched in the pockets of her smock, found a check pad and the stub of a pencil, and murmuring a fretful, 'Coming!' began to make out the bill.

'How's Jan?' the woman in the green dress inquired, over the lid of her compact. 'Are you expecting him in today?'

The girl brushed some hair from her eyes impatiently. 'He's better now. He should be in this afternoon, Miss Gilmore.'

I was about to light a cigarette, but now my hand tightened on the dormant lighter and I risked a direct look at the woman, between the sails of the windmill.

She was in her mid-thirties, not unattractive in a supercilious way. Her eyes were china blue and penetrating, her mouth a shade too large. I imagined a shrewd, restless mind at work behind the immobile face.

Her eyes met mine and I turned my head quickly away. In that instant of contact I had the feeling that hers had shown a more than casual interest in me. But I was over-receptive to impressions just then; the note in my cigarette case, and Vivien Gilmore's presence in an espresso bar which featured a Dutch doll on a bicycle in the window, was stretching coincidence to snapping point.

Through the mirror I watched the girl take the bill to Vivien Gilmore's table.

Closing her compact the latter drawled in a bored tone: 'What is it with Jan, 'flu?'

'Oh, the usual tummy trouble,' Carol replied with a sniff. 'I'll be glad when he's back. Leaving me to cope on my own here . . .'

A postman came in, flourished a bundle of mail in Carol's direction, and slapped it down on the counter at my elbow. 'Turned out nice again!' he said cheerfully.

'Has it?' Carol responded perfunctorily. 'I wouldn't know.'

I glanced casually down at the pile of mail. It seemed to be mostly bills, apart from one large buff-coloured envelope which from its bulk I assumed contained printed matter of some kind.

My attention returned abruptly to the mirror as I heard the door open and the voice of Vivien Gilmore exclaiming: 'Barbara!'

CHAPTER THIRTEEN

I heard her heels clicking, then she came into my view. She wore a close-fitting, black belted, sleeveless yellow dress, black gloves, and was hatless. She seemed a little less poised than usual as she quickly crossed to Vivien Gilmore's table.

'Sorry to be late, Vivien,' she said, a trifle edgily. 'I was held up in the traffic, then I had trouble parking the car.'

'You poor dear. I wondered what had kept you,' Vivien Gilmore drawled, glancing at her watch. 'You've just time for a coffee, Barbara. Then we *must* get down to St. Albans.'

Barbara said hesitantly: 'You think it's worth the trip?'

'Definitely,' Vivien replied lazily. 'From what I hear, the dealers' ring will be there in full force.'

As their conversation proceeded it became apparent that they were going to St. Albans to attend an auction of antique furniture. If I'd hoped to catch something that would give point to the note which had brought me to Lennard Street I was disappointed. Their talk had no more significance than the gossip you overhear from the seat behind you on a bus.

I'd been staring concentratedly into the mirror – and, of course, the inevitable happened. Barbara turned her head in my direction, frowning; then her face lit up with a smile of recognition.

'Who's that?' Vivien Gilmore said sharply as I slid off my stool and crossed over to their table.

'Hello, there!' I exclaimed. 'This *is* a surprise!'

'Yes, isn't it?' Barbara said, a shade sceptically, I thought.

Then she turned to her companion. 'Vivien, this is Mr. Frazer. We met in Amsterdam.' She glanced up at me. 'Vivien Gilmore – my partner.'

Vivien returned my greeting with a cool nod. As though sensing that her indifference had made me feel an unwelcome interloper, Barbara said quickly: 'Do sit down, Tim.'

I pulled out a chair from the table. 'I hope I haven't interrupted anything,' I said, as I sat down.

'A Board meeting,' Barbara said, with mock severity. 'The Annual General Meeting of Day and Gilmore.' She laughed. 'It's just our morning coffee break, Tim. Our antique shop is only round the corner, you know.'

I brought out my cigarette case. 'No, I didn't know. But . . . well, I'm glad it is!'

Barbara smiled at me appreciatively. 'Isn't this rather out of your way? I haven't seen you in here before.'

'It's the first time I've been here. The offices of an engineering firm I used to do business with are just down the road,' I said, offering her a cigarette. 'One of our creditors, I regret to say. I thought I'd drop in here for a coffee before seeing their accountant at eleven.'

Vivien Gilmore stood up abruptly. 'If you'll excuse me, I have to get back to the shop.'

Getting up, I said, rather stiffly: 'I'm sorry if I'm in the way.'

Barbara put out a restraining hand. 'Do sit down, Tim.

We're going down to St. Albans to see some antiques. There's no need to start for ten minutes.'

'I'll see you at the shop then, Barbara,' Vivien Gilmore said, and with a forced smile at me she left.

'Poor Vivien,' Barbara sighed, taking a cigarette from the case I'd laid on the table. 'You haven't seen her at her best, I fear. It's this Cordwell thing. She's terribly worried over the publicity – thinks it will harm our business.'

'It'll blow over,' I said as I lit her cigarette. 'I shouldn't let it get you down.'

'I won't. But the business means so much more to Vivien than to me.' She watched me light my own cigarette. 'You see, I'm not dependent on it – that is, not financially.'

'Oh – yes,' I said off-handedly. It was not a subject I could pursue, much as I should have liked to. 'As I seem to have disrupted your coffee break,' I went on, 'can I order you one now?'

'No, please I really mustn't keep Vivien waiting. She's anxious to be there for the start of the sale.' Her eyes rested on my face. 'But I'm so glad to have seen you, Tim. As a matter of fact, I tried to get you on the phone before coming here.' She glanced over at the girl polishing the coffee machine. 'It's not convenient now, but I must have a talk with you, Tim, as soon as possible.' Suddenly she looked defenceless, almost forlorn.

I said quickly: 'What time will you be back from St. Albans?'

'This evening, about seven, I imagine.'

'Then why not come round to my place for a drink when you get back?'

After a few moments' hesitation she nodded. 'All right, Tim. I'll do that. Expect me at seven-thirty.' She reached for the ashtray and slowly ground her cigarette in it. She stood up. 'And thanks a lot, Tim.'

I stood looking after her as she went past the window. I thought she must have been educated at one of those schools where the girls learn deportment by walking about for hours with books balanced on their heads. Deliberately I expelled her more glamorous aspects from my mind and wondered what it was she wanted to say to me.

A telephone ringing behind the counter reminded me of the coffee I'd left there untouched. I went across to my stool, sat down, and lifted the cup. The coffee was tepid, and I was about to call the girl over when I saw she had the telephone receiver to her ear.

'Oh, I *am* glad you're better, sir,' she was saying in a servile tone. 'All the regulars have been asking after you . . .'

Half listening to her monologue I'd decided to skip another coffee and ask for the bill, when she laid the receiver down and hurried across to the pile of mail on the counter. From this she drew out the buff envelope, tore open the flap, and took out a catalogue.

I looked down at it casually, then my eyes riveted on the gaudy cover. It was a bulb catalogue.

After a glance at it the girl hastened back to the telephone. 'That's right, sir,' she said. 'It *was* a bulb catalogue in the big envelope.' There was a pause while she listened. Then, with a final, 'It'll be ever so nice to have you back, sir,' she hung up.

I paid my bill and went out into the street. There was no reason at all why a man called Jan who ran a Dutch espresso bar shouldn't receive a bulb catalogue – there were at least twenty bowls of bulbs in the place. Equally, there was no reason why he shouldn't have a facsimile of Cordwell's Dutch doll in his window. Yet the doll plus the bulb catalogue possibly added up to more than a coincidence. But as far as I knew it was the only Dutch espresso in London. All the same, I wanted Ross's reactions to this development.

I strode briskly along the street towards the nearest call-box.

CHAPTER FOURTEEN

An hour later I was sitting opposite my chief in the smoking room of his club, sipping sherry. I smiled to myself; from the tone of my voice on the telephone he'd guessed I was in a disgruntled frame of mind, and it was typical of him to choose a stamping ground where the laws of hospitality forbade a guest to enter into a heated argument with his host.

He sipped his sherry in silence, allowing me to simmer down. Then, putting his glass on the table between us, he said conversationally, 'Well, now, Frazer? What's on your mind?'

'The Salinger Affair,' I said dryly. 'There are developments which I would like to discuss with you, sir.'

'I imagined there might be,' he said, with a wry smile. 'Suppose you bring them out where we can take a look at them.'

'I'll begin with a name,' I said, leaning back in my leather armchair. 'Ericson. I told Richards about a phone call that came through while I was in Barbara Day's flat on the night Cordwell was murdered. It was from Vivien Gilmore and she mentioned the name Ericson.'

His expression betrayed no more than polite interest.

I hesitated, then went on a little tentatively: 'Richards had obviously heard that name before.'

'It's possible,' Ross said blandly.

I leaned forward in my chair. 'It's no use, Ross,' I protested.

'You've got to trust me. I must know more about the background of the Salinger case.'

He reached for his glass and sipped his sherry thoughtfully. Then, rather to my surprise, he said: 'That's a reasonable request, Frazer. I think the time has come for me to take you more deeply into my confidence.' Returning his glass to the table he relaxed in his chair, fingering his chin. 'During the past twelve months Interpol have been very worried about a certain organisation. They've good reason for believing that the head of this organisation is someone called Ericson.'

'And this organisation,' I prompted, when he had lapsed into a frowning silence, 'what does it deal in?'

'Stolen diamonds,' he replied, coming out of his reverie. 'They're smuggled into this country from the Continent. Ericson's little group provides a highly efficient system for buying and selling them.'

'But surely,' I said, drumming my fingers on the arm of the chair, 'stolen diamonds are police business? I don't see what interest your department can have in a matter of that sort.'

'We're not directly interested in Ericson's organisation. As you say, it's purely a matter for the police,' he agreed. 'However, there *are* two angles which involve my department. Some of the diamonds smuggled into this country are industrial diamonds. Quite a brisk traffic there; mainly with the agents of foreign Powers.' He smiled. 'That is why my department comes into the picture. I've already supplied Interpol with a list of the possible agents.'

'I see,' I said untruthfully. I hadn't a clue what he was leading up to. Twisting my glass around on the table, I said: 'But where's the connection between all this and Barbara Day? Or Leo Salinger, for that matter?'

'That's the second angle in this business of the smuggled diamonds. And to me, at any rate, it's the most important angle.' His face clouded. 'Two months ago I was told that the Amsterdam police suspected Leo Salinger of being mixed up in this affair. As you can imagine, I was disturbed by this news. I trusted Leo implicitly. He'd been working with us for some time and possessed quite a lot of valuable information.' He pursed his lips ruefully, then continued, with a shrug: 'Apart from that, I pride myself on choosing the right man for the job. I didn't think I'd made a mistake about Leo – but, for security reasons, I had to check up on him. So I asked him to come to London.' He paused. 'He was on his way to the airport when he was knocked down by Barbara Day's car.'

In the silence that followed, I studied his face. This was a new Ross. I had always thought of him as a man ruthlessly dedicated to the efficient running of his department; now, for a moment, I had a glimpse of the warm, sensitive nature he normally concealed behind a mask of indifference to the feelings of his subordinates.

Vaguely touched, I said quietly: 'Was Salinger a friend of yours?'

He straightened in his chair, shooting a glance at me which was at once resentful and amused. 'A leading question, that, Frazer,' he said sharply. Then, with a small gesture of acceptance:

'I'd known him for some time. He played the piano superbly. He and his brother, Arnold, were at the Academy of Music in Amsterdam; both brilliant musicians. But, of course, I had other reasons than authentic background for employing Leo as an undercover agent. Although their mother was Dutch, the father of both the Salingers was a British naval officer.'

'Did Arnold know his brother was working for your department?'

'Of course not,' said Ross emphatically. Then his brow furrowed. 'I could wish you hadn't brought that up. I don't want to have doubts about Leo . . . But if he did tell his brother, or anyone else, he was working for our department, then I have to admit I made a mistake.' He spread his hands. 'I don't often misjudge people, Frazer; and until I have definite proof of Leo's innocence in this matter I'll have no peace of mind. Apart from my personal feelings, I don't want it on my conscience that I've let the department down.'

I smiled inwardly. This was the ruthlessly dedicated Ross. 'What happened to the metronome Salinger was carrying when he was killed?' I asked. 'Did Richards examine it?'

'The Amsterdam police handed it over to him. There were no diamonds in it, if that's what you're thinking. Nor in the one belonging to Cordwell.' He smiled blandly. 'We usually find Scotland Yard co-operative, you know, Frazer.'

'I'm glad to hear it,' I said, returning his smile. 'Then perhaps you can persuade them to hand over one of the articles they found when Cordwell was murdered?'

Ross looked at me through half closed eyes. 'Which article, Frazer? The metronome? I assure you it's been examined down to the last detail.'

'Not the metronome,' I said casually. 'I happen to be interested in the bulb catalogue.'

CHAPTER FIFTEEN

I

At six o'clock that evening I had a call from an agitated Arthur Fairlee; he was anxious to know if I could meet him in half an hour in the upstairs bar at *The Antelope*. Remembering that I had an appointment with Barbara at my flat for seven-thirty I was about to make an excuse, then I had second thoughts. I decided not to risk my talk with Barbara being interrupted by a jealous Fairlee banging on my door. So I agreed to meet him for a couple of quick drinks.

He was standing at the bar, fidgeting with a gin and lime, when I arrived.

'We'll have to make this snappy, Fairlee,' I warned him after he had ordered my small whisky and ginger ale, 'I've an appointment at seven-thirty.'

From behind the spectacles the pale blue eyes quizzed my face curiously. 'With Bar—' he began, then swiftly covered his lapse. '. . . With that blasted policeman?'

I shook my head. 'What made you think that, Fairlee?'

'Damned fellow's been hounding me. Had an hour of him at my office this afternoon.' He pursed his lips petulantly. 'Questioning me about Barbara's relationship with this Cordwell fellow.'

'But she's already told him that she hardly knew the man,' I said evasively. It seemed I was to be subjected to the boredom of allaying the suspicions of a jealous fiancé.

'Yes, I know. But for some reason or another this Inspector doesn't seem to believe anything he's told.' His prominent Adam's apple wobbled convulsively. 'Frazer, you were with Barbara when she met Cordwell at that café place.'

'Yes,' I said, trying to keep a note of exasperation out of my voice.

The Adam's apple worked vigorously, then he rushed on: 'Did *you* get the impression that they might have met before?'

'Of course they'd seen each other before. They were staying at the same hotel.'

'Yes, I know. I didn't mean that.'

Without disguising my annoyance I said: 'What *did* you mean, Fairlee?'

He looked into his glass. 'Did you think when they were at the café that they behaved – well, as though they were on particularly friendly terms?'

It was a question I'd asked myself at the time. 'No, I didn't,' I said, wondering if this answer were not as much to reassure myself as Fairlee. 'But I'm not Miss Day's fiancé, of course. You would have been a better judge of her reactions.'

'Now, don't get the wrong impression about Barbara,' he said hastily. 'Of course, I trust her. But it's this questioning by the police that's so upsetting.' He slammed his glass down on the bar counter. 'They've even questioned Vivien Gilmore!'

'Why?' I asked sharply.

'Lord knows!' he said gloomily. 'I haven't the slightest idea, old man.'

Then why, I thought, did he offer me that piece of information? I decided to do some fishing myself. 'Does Miss Gilmore spend her holidays in Amsterdam?'

'Good Lord, no! She can't stand the place. I remember her telling me . . .' He broke off, then said slowly; 'Why did you ask me that?'

I shrugged. 'I thought perhaps that was why the police had questioned her.'

'Ah, naturally you would. Very perspicacious of you, old man.' He smiled thinly. 'No, Vivien loathes Holland. Frankly, I agree with her. Damn dull hole, if you ask me.' He picked up his glass and sipped his drink before going on: 'Why Barbara should want to go there, after what happened a couple of months back, defeats me.'

I summoned up a polite show of interest. 'Something unpleasant?'

'Very,' he said, his eyes never leaving my face. 'She ran over a man in Amsterdam; a chap called Salinger. He was killed, poor devil.'

'Good God!' I exclaimed.

'Nasty business. Still, it wasn't her fault, apparently.' He glanced at his watch. 'Good heavens, is that the time?' He finished his drink hurriedly, 'Just remembered I have an appointment, Frazer. Quite forgot it, chatting away here. Mind if I

dash, old boy? But, of course, you have an appointment, too.'
With rather too elaborate casualness he added: 'If you're going
anywhere in the direction of the West End . . .'

'My car's outside,' I cut in on him. 'Thanks, all the same.'

'Well, good-bye, Frazer.' Without offering a hand he turned,
then swung back. 'Oh – er – if you should run into Barbara at
any time . . . I'd rather you didn't mention our conversation. I'd
hate her to think I was checking up on her.'

I promised, with mental reservations, to keep everything
under my hat, and with a 'That's a good chap' he moved over
to the staircase.

Dawdling over my drink, to give him time to drive off before
I left, I considered our conversation. I had a feeling that it was
not entirely jealousy that had prompted Fairlee to arrange our
meeting. No doubt he was suspicious of Barbara's relationship
with Cordwell. But was there more to it than that? He'd said
two things that puzzled me. One was the reference to Vivien
Gilmore having been questioned by the police. He'd brought
that up, then dropped it immediately I began to get curious.
The other was his telling me about Salinger being run over by
Barbara's car. He'd been watching me closely when he mentioned
it. He could, of course, have been pumping me to find out how
friendly *I* was with Barbara. It could have been that, I decided,
finishing my drink; and the reference to the questioning of
Vivien Gilmore could have been no more than a jealous man's
masochistic desire to torture himself over his fiancée's friendship
with another male. Dismissing Fairlee as a frustrated Romeo,
I went down to my car, and drove back to my flat.

2

Parked in the mews, outside my door, was a Morris Minor saloon of uncertain age. Leaning against it, smoking a cigarette, was a long figure whom I recognised with a muttered imprecation.

As I got out of my car Richards said: 'A drink, for the love of Allah! I've been kicking my heels for half an hour, waiting for you.'

'There *is* a new-fangled invention called the telephone,' I said, grinning at him. 'It'll have to be a quick drink. I'm expecting a visitor in ten minutes.'

In my living room, as I handed him a whisky and soda, he said sardonically: 'Your visitor wouldn't be Barbara Day, by any chance?'

I turned back to the drinks table. 'Talking of her,' I said, with a forced laugh, 'I've just had a chat with Fairlee.'

'That sounds intriguing. What did he want?'

'Oh, nothing really. Just wanted to get a load of jealousy out of his system.' I returned with my drink. 'God knows what Barbara Day sees in him!'

Richards looked at me quizzically for a long moment, then with a murmured, 'Skol!' sipped his drink.

I began to pace the room, as much to escape his amused stare as anything. Forget it, I told myself. What if Barbara does come while he's here? All right she's a damned attractive woman; but that doesn't mean Richards' innuendoes should get under my skin.

'I heard you saw Ross this afternoon,' he was saying.

I nodded. 'Quite a frank talk, actually. It cleared the air, if nothing else.'

'I understand you've asked for the bulb catalogue that was found with Cordwell?'

I fiddled with an ornament on my writing desk.

'He didn't mention why you wanted it,' Richards went on, his tone adding a question mark to the statement.

'He didn't ask me, for one thing,' I said coolly, rather resenting his persistence. 'And if he had I couldn't really have told him. For your information, I'm playing a hunch.'

'Good luck to you,' Richards said, returning my smile. 'By the way, you're not the only one who's getting inquisitive about Cordwell's possessions. Barbara Day asked Trueman if she could have a private view of the film they found on him. They ran it through for her this morning.'

'Rather an odd request,' I said, genuinely puzzled. 'Did she give any reason?'

'No. But I think I can supply one.' He frowned into his glass. 'She's obviously getting very, *very* curious about you, Frazer.' He paused, then looked up with a quizzical smile. 'It *is* Barbara Day you're expecting, isn't it?'

'Well, yes, it is,' I said defensively. 'Although the invitation was at her request.'

'That doesn't surprise me. I'd take a bet she wants to discuss the film with you.' He shook his head at me, chidingly. 'That film is going to take a devil of a lot of explaining away. I've seen it. And, in my opinion, you overdid those shots of her.'

'It's easily explainable. I've already told her she only came into the film because I wanted to include a pretty woman in my memories of Amsterdam.'

'Is that so?' Richards murmured. 'I'd say you were including Amsterdam in your memories of Barbara Day.'

He was still smiling cynically as he drew back the window curtain. 'And here is the star of your film, making a personal appearance. And in a Rover 3 Litre, too.' He dropped the curtain. 'Do you mind if I fade out of the picture into your bedroom?'

The thought of Richards listening in to what promised to be an embarrassing conversation didn't greatly appeal to me. But I was caught on the wrong foot. 'It's the door on your left,' I said curtly.

'Make it sound convincing,' he advised, 'but try to find out if she suspects anything.'

I nodded as the door bell rang.

3

She'd changed into the suit she'd been wearing the first time I saw her. But, as I followed her into the living room, I thought she looked less at ease than she had then.

'I'm sorry, Tim, but I'm terribly on edge,' she said, over her shoulder. 'That detective was waiting for me outside my flat when I got back from St. Albans. This cat and mouse business really is preposterous. I'm sick and tired of answering the same old questions. I must have told him a dozen times I've never heard of this – what's his name? – Oh, Ericson.'

As I looked down at the dark brown eyes ablaze with indignation I refrained with difficulty from challenging her, there and then, with Vivien Gilmore's telephone message. I think it was only the thought of Richards listening behind the bedroom door that deterred me. Abruptly, I turned, and went over to the drinks table.

'Do sit down, Barbara. What can I get you?'

'Please, if you have it, a brandy and ginger ale.' She sank into an easy chair. 'What a day it's been! Vivien, then that dreadful Inspector, then Arthur . . .' Her tone lightened. 'He hasn't phoned you, has he?'

Keeping my back to her I clinked bottles while I made up my mind whether to tell her or not. 'No,' I lied. 'No, he hasn't.'

'Well, that's one mercy,' she said, with a short laugh. 'Perhaps he's stopped being suspicious at last.'

When I came back with the drinks she smiled up at me. I took my whisky and soda to the chair opposite hers and sat down.

'This is definitely what I needed,' she said. 'Now, I suppose I should tell you why I wanted to see you.' She looked at me from under half closed eyelids. 'I've seen your film, Tim. The one they found on Cordwell. The police ran it through for me.'

'Not exactly a professional job, I'm afraid,' I said easily. 'It was a first attempt, you know. I'd only bought the camera just before I went away.'

Her eyes widened. 'For a beginner the shots were remarkably

good – particularly the ones of me.' She twirled the stem of her glass between her fingers, then demanded bluntly: 'Why were you following me in Amsterdam, Tim?'

'Following you?' I repeated. I hadn't expected her to be quite so quick off the mark, and was momentarily at a loss.

'There can't be any other explanation. Although the Inspector only seemed to recognise me in one or two shots, I caught a glimpse of myself in at least six others.' Her eyes narrowed. 'I simply can't believe that we both happened, by chance, to be in those places at the same time.'

There didn't seem much purpose in continuing to deny her accusation. 'All right,' I said, with a half smile, 'I *was* following you.'

Her knuckles whitened as her fingers tightened on her glass. It was a moment before she spoke. 'Why?'

'If you insist on knowing,' I said, feeling slightly ridiculous, 'it was because you are . . . well, an extremely attractive woman.'

'But why follow me?' she persisted. 'You'd met me on the plane. There was no reason why you couldn't have asked me to go out with you.'

'You'd made it very plain to me that you were engaged. I can take a hint as well as most people.'

She relaxed in the chair. 'So you just kept a respectful distance,' she murmured. 'That's rather touching.'

'You sound relieved,' I said sharply, in an attempt to discover whether she believed my explanation.

'As a matter of fact, I am,' she said imperturbably. 'I thought you must be a private investigator or something.'

'Me!' I laughed. 'I've told you, I'm an engineer.'

'I don't know why I should have thought that. But strange things have been happening since . . .' She fluttered a hand. 'Oh, let's forget it. You're not a private detective, and that's all that matters.'

'I can't let you get away with it as easily as that,' I said lightly. 'Not after having practically accused me of spying on you. What are these strange things that have been happening to you?'

She bit her lip. 'I hate going over all this.' She closed her eyes. 'I killed a man.'

I tried to appear suitably shocked.

Her eyes opened, and looked directly into my face. 'In a car accident in Amsterdam. His name was Leo Salinger. Oh, it was his own fault – that was proved at the inquest – but that didn't make me feel any better about it. I tried to contact his family, even consulted a solicitor to trace them, but without results. I just came up against a blank wall.'

'That *is* strange. He must have had some relatives.'

'Tim,' she said, suddenly leaning forward in her chair. 'You don't think there's a connection between Cordwell's murder and my car accident?'

'I don't see how there could be,' I said, watching her. 'Do you?'

'Not unless Cordwell had known Salinger. Cordwell *had* been in Amsterdam before, you remember.'

'Yes, he said he had all his possessions stolen.' I gripped the arm of my chair. 'What are you driving at, Barbara?'

'Oh, I don't know – I'm so confused by it all.' She brushed the back of her hand across her forehead. 'Can't we talk about something else now?'

'How about another drink? You've finished that one.'

She glanced at the watch on her wrist. 'No, I really must fly now. Vivien and I have to take some furniture down to Surrey. We're supposed to be there by nine.'

'Don't you ever let up?' I said, trying not to sound too curious. 'I never seem to be able to pin you down. It's either a five-minute drink or a two-minute coffee.'

She made a little face at me, and I went on: 'There was that first date I had with you . . .' I left the sentence unfinished, hoping she would give me a lead-in to my real purpose.

She shuddered. 'That dreadful evening; and I had so looked forward to it.'

'I meant to ask you this before,' I said casually, getting up and taking our empty glasses to the drinks table. 'It's always puzzled me why you invited me to your flat that night, Barbara.'

'But I've told you – to meet my fiancé.'

I crossed the room and looked down at her. 'He's almost psychopathically jealous. I should have thought the one thing you'd have wanted to avoid would be introducing a man you'd met on holiday.'

'That's the whole point,' she said earnestly. 'I'd mentioned meeting you. If I hadn't asked you to the flat after that, he'd have suspected there'd been something more between us than just a casual acquaintance.'

'I suppose he would,' I had to agree.

She stood up, smoothing the jacket of her suit. 'I'm so glad we've had this talk, Tim. I hated to feel I couldn't trust you.'

'And you do now?'

Her eyes misted. 'You know I do,' she said softly,

She was very close to me now; her face raised to mine. As I involuntarily made a movement towards her she placed a restraining hand against my chest. 'Tim, why did you ask me about the invitation to my flat?'

I smiled at her. 'You've explained it all now, Barbara.'

'And you're not suspicious of me?'

I wasn't thinking very clearly at that instant. 'Suspicious of you? Of course not. Why should I be?'

Her hand dropped to her side, and she sighed deeply. 'Everyone else seems to be.'

Looking down at the head dropped so close to my chin I had an almost overwhelming desire to stroke the jet black hair. Then I remembered Richards. I stepped away from her. 'You mustn't keep dear Vivien waiting,' I said, with a light laugh.

She looked at me for a moment, rather dazedly, then smiled. 'Thanks, Tim. I'd completely forgotten her.'

The spell was broken and, as I ushered her out into the hall, we were two normal people exchanging conventional phrases after a social drink.

When I came back to the living room Richards was squirting soda on to a whisky. 'Sorry to abuse your hospitality, but my tongue was sticking to the roof of my mouth.'

'Mine too,' I said, with a laugh I hoped didn't sound too

embarrassed. 'Her refusing another drink rather cramped my style.'

'So I gathered,' he said dryly. 'Oh, by the way, here's the bulb catalogue you wanted.' Taking it from his jacket pocket, he handed it to me.

I flipped the pages. 'Let's hope my hunch pays off.' I strolled over to the drinks table. 'Well, what did you make of it all?'

He was in the middle of the room, his feet planted wide. 'Can I give you a piece of advice, Frazer?'

Unstoppering the whisky decanter, I said: 'About not mixing business with other things?'

'Something like that.'

Why the hell must he always act the schoolmaster, I thought irritably, giving myself a stiffer than usual whisky. I lifted the glass, smiling at him.

He said, quietly: 'But you can take care of yourself, can't you, Frazer?'

'I can take care of myself, Richards.'

'A lot of other people have said the same thing.' He tossed back his whisky. 'Perhaps Leo Salinger said it. Who knows?'

CHAPTER SIXTEEN

I

After I had breakfasted next morning I lit a cigarette and went over the bulb catalogue, page by page. I could find nothing which might conceal a cryptic message; no underlined letters that could have been the basis of a code. It was just like any other garden catalogue.

I skimmed through the names of the tulips. Flamingo, Snowstorm, Gold Lace, Velvet King, Blue Gem, and other exotic names calculated to make the green fingers of a gardener itch. If I'd had a garden I could have had a two-tone collection of 50 at 11/6d. – if I'd had a garden. I hadn't; but I had a hunch that I could plant the catalogue where the tulips on the cover would not bloom unseen.

As Mrs. Glover was clearing away the breakfast things she said, in an innocent tone intended to conceal her undying curiosity. 'Was that lady who was here last night the one who phoned in the morning, Mr. Frazer?'

'You should keep up with the times, Mrs. Glover. *Men* use perfume these days.' Then I did a quick double-take. 'Did she leave her name?'

Mrs. Glover came down from the heights of indignation reluctantly. 'All she said was, were you in? When I said, no you wasn't, she hung up quick.' Mrs. Glover smiled innocently. 'Could it have been a *woman* policeman, do you suppose, sir?'

I said yes, it was the one who was teaching me Judo. We decided to call it a draw; and I went down into the mews, got my car out of the garage, and drove to Lennard Street.

After parking my car I walked quickly to *The Dyke* coffee bar.

Time might almost have stood still since I'd been there last. The sole customer, at the same table she'd occupied previously, in the green dress she'd worn the day before, was Vivien Gilmore. The one difference was that, instead of the string-haired girl, a man now stood behind the counter. He was short and thick-set, with black hair growing low on his forehead. His eyes were deep-set under bushy eyebrows. His heavy jowl was already showing 'five o'clock shadow'.

As I came in Vivien Gilmore called across to him: 'My bill, please, Jan.'

I went over to her table, and stood with my hand hesitating on the back of a chair. 'Good morning, Miss Gilmore.'

She glanced guardedly up at me. 'Oh, good morning,' she drawled, assuming what, for her, was a friendly smile. 'Won't you sit down?'

As I pulled out the chair Jan lumbered over from the bar. 'Nice weather again today, Miss Gilmore,' he said, with a heavy Dutch accent. Although I didn't look up at him I knew from the direction of his voice that he was scrutinising me. He was pawing up the money for the bill with a hairy hand when I looked up at him.

'A coffee, please,' I said, suddenly catching his gaze. 'Won't you join me, Miss Gilmore?'

'I'm just going,' she said, snapping her handbag shut. 'But thanks all the same.'

After another speculative glance at me Jan moved back to the counter.

'Barbara not coming in today?' I said, turning to Vivien.

'I'm afraid not. We're frantically busy.' She pulled on a glove. 'And, to crown everything, the police have been to the shop again this morning.'

I clicked my tongue sympathetically.

'I've read about murder cases, police investigations, and people being questioned,' she went on. 'But never in my wildest dreams did I imagine it would be anything like this!' She gave an expressive shrug. 'That Inspector person is like a terrier. I'm sure he'd use any sort of torture if he could get the right answers. As though I'd know whether Cordwell had any appointments with a man called Margetson!'

I scratched my chin. 'Was that the name? I thought it was Ericson.'

'Oh, Ericson – was that it?' She looked at me blankly for a moment. 'The name doesn't mean a thing to me. And why should it? I'd never even heard of Cordwell until I saw his name in the paper; so how on earth am I supposed to know he had an appointment with . . .'

'Ericson,' I suggested quietly.

'Oh, I couldn't care less what his name is.' She rose. 'I really must go now.'

I stood up. 'By the way, Miss Gilmore – you didn't phone me yesterday morning, by any chance?'

'What an extraordinary question,' she drawled, eyeing me almost insolently. 'I scarcely know you.'

'Nor I you,' I said with a smile. 'Whoever it was didn't leave a name. My daily woman took the call, but she didn't recognise the voice . . . I happen to have a rather keen ear for voices, Miss Gilmore,' I added, looking at her steadily, and mentally recalling the first time I'd listened to her penetrating voice on the telephone in Barbara's flat. 'Yes, I've a very good memory for voices.'

She held my gaze for a second or two, without answering. Then, with a hard little smile, she said: 'I mustn't keep Barbara waiting, Mr. Frazer.' She exchanged a glance with Jan, then sauntered out of the coffee bar.

I sat down and cautiously looked across at the man behind the counter. He had drawn my coffee from the espresso machine and was about to bring it over to me. I took the bulb catalogue from my pocket, opened it, and turned the pages slowly, as though absorbed in the selection of tulips for my garden.

As he placed the coffee in front of me I held the catalogue so that the brightly coloured cover was directly under his eyes.

'Thanks,' I said, acknowledging the coffee with an upward glance.

His eyes flickered from the catalogue to my face; then a hairy hand rose to his jowl, fingering it thoughtfully.

'Are you interested in bulbs, Jan?' I asked, meaningly.

His hand continued to stroke his jowl. 'When did *you* arrive?'

'You haven't answered my question,' I said coolly.

He gave me another long, speculative look, then nodded, more to himself than to me, and returned to the bar. He peered beneath the counter, took something out, returned without a word, and slid it on to the table in front of me. It was a bulb catalogue exactly like Cordwell's . . .

A stubby finger reached across and pointed at a sticker on the cover. 'This is a new one,' Jan said heavily. 'It's up to date.'

My eyes focused on the sticker. *International Bulb Importers*, it read. *London Agents: Gordon Dempsey, 43a Long Acre, E.C.4.*

2

When I left *The Dyke*, with the two bulb catalogues tucked under my arm, I made a bee-line for the telephone kiosk, only to find that I hadn't even one penny amongst the change in my pocket. A fruit barrow that I'd noticed previously parked outside the espresso bar was now at the kerb beside the call-box. I went across to it.

'I wonder if you could change that for me?' I asked, handing the barrow boy a sixpence. 'I'm out of coppers for the phone.'

'Anythin' to oblige, guv!' he said with an engaging grin. 'There we are! Three an' three is six.'

As I thanked him he looked round cautiously, then said in a low voice: 'Want to do yerself a bit of good, guv? Then don't forget "Fantasy". It's in the two-thirty. Best tip of the week, guv!'

I smiled and nodded my head, then went into the call-box.

I looked up Gordon Dempsey in the directory, and dialled his number. After listening for a full minute to the burring at the other end I hung up, and as it was almost noon I decided to have a snack lunch before phoning Dempsey again.

As I left the call-box the barrow boy was grinning broadly. 'Don't forget – Fantasy in the two-thirty, guv!' he reminded me. 'You're on a winner there!'

I flipped my hand in acknowledgement, then paused, biting my lip thoughtfully. I hadn't noticed it before, but now I thought there was something vaguely familiar about the trim, fair-haired figure. I shrugged; he was just a rather sprucer than normal barrow boy.

I returned to my car, drove down to the Brompton Road, and parked in a side street near the Brompton Oratory, beside a pub which I believe was called *The Grapes* – a Victorian collector's-piece, with enormous wall mirrors and mahogany fittings. Here I had a slice of veal and ham pie, potato salad, and a tankard of bitter at the bar counter. I'd bought a midday paper from the newspaper seller outside and I scanned it for any further developments in the Cordwell murder. All I found was a buried news item which proved no more informative than is customary when the police are running round in circles. Reading between the lines, it seemed that Detective-Inspector Trueman was up against a blank wall.

Out of curiosity I turned to the racing page. My barrow boy's 'hot tip' looked as cold as the veal and ham pie. No horse named Fantasy was listed among the runners for the two-thirty that afternoon.

After lunch I drove in the direction of Long Acre, stopping twice at call-boxes in the attempt to telephone Dempsey, but with no result. Eventually, I decided that he must be a three-hour-lunch man, left my car at the Lex Garage in Brewer Street, and went to a news theatre.

It was five o'clock before I made contact with Dempsey. Then, at the first ring, the receiver was lifted and a fruity voice said: 'International Bulb Importers.'

'Dempsey speaking,' the voice said when I asked for him by name.

I tried to sound convincing as I said: 'I'm interested in buying some bulbs, Mr. Dempsey. Your firm was recommended by a friend of mine.'

There was a pause of a few seconds at the other end, then the voice asked guardedly: 'What's the name of this friend?'

'Ericson,' I said, my hand tightening on the receiver.

I could almost sense Dempsey's nod as he responded at once, quite matter-of-factly, with: 'I see. And what's *your* name?'

A telephone directory was open on the ledge at my elbow. I glanced at it and gave the first name that met my eye. 'Scott – Norman Scott. You don't know me.'

'No, I don't.' Dempsey paused, then asked: 'Have you got a catalogue?'

'Of course,' I said easily. 'Otherwise I couldn't have phoned you.'

'That's right.' He appeared to have swallowed my story. 'I'll be in my office for the next half-hour,' he said decisively. 'And don't forget to bring the catalogue with you.'

I assured him I shouldn't forget, and rang off.

There wasn't much sense in picking up my car and then touring Long Acre searching for an unoccupied parking meter. So I walked briskly through the side-streets and was outside Dempsey's office building in three minutes.

It was not exactly impressive. A hand-painted sign in the entrance informed me that International Bulb Importers occupied an office on the first floor. I climbed the wooden stairs and went down a dismal passage until I came to a glass-panelled door marked 'International Bulb Importers. London and Hilversum.'

At my knock the fruity voice I'd heard on the telephone called: 'Come in.'

3

I opened the door and entered a room carpeted with much-worn linoleum. The damp-streaked walls were partly concealed by faded posters depicting Holland, and, slightly askew, a calendar advertising a fertiliser. The furniture consisted of one wooden-backed visitor's-chair, a filing cabinet, and a desk. Behind this sat a middle-aged man, eating a sandwich with obvious relish. His face was as round and colourless as a December full moon; his sandy hair was parted just above one ear and sparsely combed across a bald dome.

'Mr. Scott?' he inquired, through a mouth full of sandwich. I nodded, and he waved the sandwich at the wooden-backed chair. 'Have you got the catalogue?'

I'd taken the precaution of leaving Cordwell's copy in my car. I now produced the one Jan had given me and put it on the desk. Dempsey pulled it over to him, scrutinised the sticker, then looked over at me inquiringly.

For a moment I was nonplussed, realising that what I said next was probably the pay-off. I decided to throw the ball back into his court. 'I haven't quite made up my mind about which tulips . . .' I broke off with a slight smile.

Apparently I'd said the right thing. Dempsey nodded, took another bite at his sandwich, and with a splutter of crumbs began to reel off a list of names. 'Well, we've got Piccadilly, Red Parrot, Fantasy, Octavius, Hilversum Red . . .'

My mind flashed back to the barrow boy! With forced composure I said, 'I think I'll take some – Fantasy.'

He gulped down the remainder of the sandwich and explored a tooth with his tongue while he studied my face. 'How many?'

It seemed I'd backed a winner with the first half of the barrow boy's tip – Fantasy. Now I gambled that the time of the race was significant. 'Let me see . . . I should say . . . well, two-thirty.'

Dempsey's small mouth stretched into a smile. 'All right, Mr. Scott,' he agreed affably. 'What would you say to joining me in a cup of coffee before we get down to business?'

What I needed at that moment was a double Scotch. Also, I wanted to avoid answering questions. 'Thanks all the same,' I said hesitantly, 'but why waste time by going out now?'

'I keep it on the premises,' he replied genially, leaning back and pulling out a drawer of the filing cabinet. 'Doctor's orders.

"Feed your ulcer, Mr. Dempsey," he said. "Have a bite of something and a hot coffee every two hours." He produced two saucerless breakfast cups and a Thermos flask from the drawer and placed them on his desk. 'Hot as the devil, sweet as sin, eh, Mr. Scott?' He chuckled, unscrewing the lid of the Thermos and pouring the steaming liquid into the cups. Passing one across to me he went on cheerfully; 'Now then, we'll get down to business.'

He took a key-ring from his pocket, selected a key, and unlocked a drawer in his desk. The palms of my hands grew damp as I watched him.

'There we are!' he said, bringing out an object and placing it on the desk beside the Thermos flask.

I had last seen its exact counterpart beside the dead body of Cordwell . . . Dempsey moved the gaily decorated metronome on to his blotter and beamed at me expansively.

4

The barrow boy's tip had produced the rabbit out of the hat! Now I felt as foolish as the member of the audience who has accepted the conjurer's invitation to step onto the stage. I accepted my role as the stooge and smiled aimlessly.

Like a cloud crossing the moon, the glow faded from Dempsey's face. 'Well, Mr. Scott . . . ?' he prompted.

At that instant the telephone rang. Without taking his eyes from mine he reached slowly for the receiver.

'International Bulb Importers.'

Whoever it was at the other end wasted no time on preliminaries. I couldn't catch any of the flood of words, but I realised that the voice was a woman's. Dempsey listened intently, his mouth pursed, and I knew that the tense, urgent voice on the phone was warning him about me. Occasionally I thought I could detect a note in the voice which seemed familiar.

Whilst the call lasted I assumed an air of detachment, as one does when the person one is with takes a phone call. But I knew I wouldn't get away with it.

There was a sudden click in the earpiece, and with maddening deliberation Dempsey replaced the receiver.

Half rising, and with every nerve alert, I mentally calculated the distance to the door.

'Just a minute, Mr. Scott,' Dempsey said menacingly. 'Or should I say . . . Mr. Frazer?' His hand snatched open his centre drawer and a gun was pointing at me before I had a chance to rise from the chair.

My lips were dry but I attempted a feeble smile. 'Not very efficient, are you, Dempsey? The safety catch is on.'

As his eyes dropped to the gun I grabbed the coffee cup and flung the contents in his face. He gave a small, choking scream and, dropping the gun, clawed at his face. Sweeping the gun from the desk to the floor, I snatched up the metronome and ran from the room.

CHAPTER SEVENTEEN

I

A taxi was dropping a fare as I came out of the office building. I was in it before the driver had put his flag up, and directed him to the Lex Garage in Brewer Street.

Immediately I'd retrieved my car I drove to Lennard Street, cursing the rush-hour traffic. I wanted to catch the barrow boy before he packed up. I knew now why I'd experienced that vague sense of familiarity when I'd seen him that morning. In the moment Dempsey had pulled the gun on me a chain of images had flashed through my mind: looking down the muzzle of a gun; the blow on the back of my head; my recovering consciousness; the neat, fair-haired figure of a man slipping a note into my cigarette case . . . I was certain now that the barrow boy and the man who had left the note were one and the same person.

Turning into Lennard Street I thought for a moment that I'd missed him. Then I spotted the barrow at the far end. I braked behind it, got out, and went up to him.

He had his back to me as I said: 'Thanks for the tip – it came off.'

He turned an unfamiliar sallow face towards me, waggling the stub of a cigarette between thin lips. 'What's that, mate? Mistook me for someone else, 'ave yer?'

'Oh, I'm sorry!' I said, with a laugh. 'A pound of apples, please.'

He eyed me as though I were a drunk, decided I wasn't, put four apples in a bag, and tossed it onto his scales. 'That'll be two bob, guv.'

I took a five-pound note out of my wallet. 'Where's the other chap who was on the barrow this morning?' I asked.

'Oh, 'im. 'E's 'aving a night orf,' he said. Then he scratched his head. 'Ain't you got nothin' smaller than that?'

'You needn't bother about change,' I said, waving the fiver at him. 'That is, if you tell me where that other man is.'

'What you take me for?' he said nastily. 'Go on – scarper!'

He came round eventually, after I'd shown him an old business card that I had in my wallet, and persuaded him that the other man was an old schoolfellow.

'Well, this chap, 'e just come up to me, see – and 'e give me a tenner for the loan of me barrow! Says 'e was an author writin' a book about barrow boys. To tell yer the truth, mate, I wondered what he was up to, so I kept me eye on 'im from round the corner, see. 'E don't make no move to serve no-one! Then today I see 'im givin' you the nod.' He wiped his nose with the sleeve of his jacket. 'Beats me, guv!'

'Will you be seeing him again?'

'Dunno. Might see 'im in the boozer – he's been in there the last couple o' nights . . .'

'Give him this card if you do see him,' I said, handing the card over with the five-pound note. 'It's got my phone number on it. Tell him to give me a ring.'

'Right-o!' He stuck the fiver in his waistcoat pocket, grinning at me. 'Cor! The Missis won't believe a flipping word of this!'

2

As I turned out of Lennard Street I noticed a slim, angry-looking figure in a bowler, waving an umbrella at the stream of occupied taxis. I pulled in to the kerb beside him.

'Want a lift, Fairlee?' I called through the open window of my car. 'You'll never get a taxi at this hour.'

He blinked myopically at me for a moment, then gave me one of his rare smiles. 'Oh, it's you, Frazer. It would be jolly helpful if you could drop me off at Hyde Park Corner.'

I said, untruthfully, that I was going in that direction, and reached over and unlatched the door.

'I do appreciate this, old man,' he said, sliding into the seat beside me. 'What a stroke of luck you should happen to be passing.' From the rather sly way in which he said this I had the idea that he was trying to pump me.

'Yes, it is, isn't it?' I said innocently. 'I came down that street to short circuit the rush-hour traffic.' I drew away from the kerb. 'I must remember that short cut for future occasions.'

'Yes, the taxis use it quite a bit,' he said indifferently.

My offer of a lift had not been entirely altruistic. I'd been as curious about his reason for being in Lennard Street as he had obviously been about mine. 'Have you just come from Miss Day's shop?' I asked conversationally.

'As a matter of fact, I have,' he said sombrely. 'I wanted to have a talk with Barbara about a visit I had from that detective this afternoon. Unfortunately, she wasn't available.'

'Bad luck,' I murmured, and casually inquired what Trueman wanted to know this time.

'He's got it into his wooden head that I can give him some information about a man called Ericson.'

'And can you?'

'No, of course I can't! Never heard of the chap.' His emphasis brought on a brief spell of asthmatic coughing. When he'd got over that, he said: 'Has he been questioning you about Ericson?'

'He did ask me whether I knew him.'

Fairlee seemed more exasperated than ever. 'Vivien tells me he's been hounding her, too. Why he should be so keen on trying to pin some knowledge of Ericson on to all of us defeats me.'

'All of *us*?' I said sharply. 'Who do you mean, exactly, Fairlee?'

'Well, isn't it obvious?' he said peevishly. 'You, me, Barbara, Vivien – he doesn't trust any of us. I must say it's a fine state of affairs that I, a reputable stockbroker, should be subjected to the indignity of being cross-examined by that idiot of a policeman! And in connection with a murder, of all things!'

From then until we reached Hyde Park Corner I had to listen to a monologue on the impeccable life of Arthur Fairlee, and when I finally said good-bye to him I found myself wondering whether Barbara had any inkling of what she was letting herself in for.

Half an hour later, sitting opposite Barbara Day in the American bar at the Dorchester, I again thought how incredible it was that so glamorous a personality should be engaged to a man like Fairlee. It had been her idea that we should meet for a quick drink and she'd sounded anxious on the telephone.

Lighting her cigarette, I said: 'A quick drink – that's all it ever is, eh, Barbara?'

'I'm sorry, Tim.' Impulsively, her hand touched mine, then was as quickly withdrawn. 'But I *have* to meet Vivien in half an hour, I've been out of the shop since lunch.' Her face clouded. 'That's why I wanted to see you, Tim – about what happened this afternoon.'

I fingered the stem of my sherry glass. 'Well . . . ?'

'I went back to my flat at lunch-time to change. I'd spilt some coffee on the dress I was wearing. So I hurried into the flat without paying much attention to anything. Then I noticed that some things weren't in their usual places, so I had a look over the entire flat. It wasn't very obvious, but a drawer in a bureau wasn't quite closed; the kitchen door was open and I'm positive I closed it this morning . . .' Her eyes held mine. 'Tim, somebody has been searching my flat.'

'Was anything stolen?' I asked tentatively.

She shook her head. 'That's what puzzles me. There was some money in a drawer, and some jewellery on my dressing table. Oh, nothing very expensive, but a thief wouldn't have ignored it.'

'It sounds as though whoever got into your flat was looking for something,' I said slowly. 'Maybe letters, or a document of some kind – does that suggest anything to you?'

'But I haven't anything of that sort that could possibly—' She caught her breath. 'You mean anything that could be used to blackmail me?'

'Oh, now, just a minute, Barbara,' I said deprecatingly. 'I wasn't implying you had anything . . .'

'Of course you weren't, Tim,' she said lightly. Then her expression changed; she said, with a frown, quite suddenly: 'Cordwell was a blackmailer.'

I nearly snapped the stem of my glass in two. 'How do you know that?' I demanded.

'As soon as I was sure my flat had been entered I thought I'd better telephone Inspector Trueman. He came round to the flat, but he didn't seem particularly interested in what I had to tell him. Then, for some reason I can't fathom, he proceeded to tell me that Cordwell was a blackmailer.'

I frowned. 'It's not like him to give information away.'

'He was watching me all the time in a shifty sort of way. I felt he was hinting at something connected with Cordwell's blackmailing activities.' Her mouth trembled. 'I had a horrible feeling he was hinting that Cordwell and I . . .' She hesitated.

'Were running a blackmail racket?' Laughing, I shook my head. 'Trueman's like all policemen; they always try to push you on to the defensive. What else did he tell you?'

'Ask me, you mean,' she said wearily. 'He wanted to know if Cordwell actually smoked cigars.'

'Very pungent cigars, from what I remember of that evening at *De Kroon*,' I said casually. Then suddenly the oddity of Trueman's question hit me like the blast of a furnace. 'What was he getting at? Did he give you any clue?'

'He said they'd searched Cordwell's room at his hotel in the Cromwell Road. Apparently they found several boxes of cigars in his suitcase. Full boxes.' She shrugged. 'I can't think why he imagined it would interest me; but he seemed to expect me to collapse or something.'

'I think you *are* rather letting your imagination run away with you,' I said, my mind busy with Trueman's motives. 'Still, I'm glad you told me all this, Barbara,' I added. 'You know you can always unload your worries about this Cordwell business onto me, don't you?'

'Yes,' she said softly. Her eyes dropped to her glass and she hesitated, twirling it along the table.

'Go on . . .' I prompted. 'There's something on your mind.'

'Oh, well . . . I was just wondering why I didn't phone Arthur when all this happened . . .'

'Well, why didn't you, Barbara?'

'I don't know. I didn't think of it. I thought of you . . .' She raised her eyes to mine. 'I just picked up the phone and found myself dialling your number.'

I could almost hear Richards laughing sardonically. 'Talking of Arthur,' I said, 'I met your fiancé just before you telephoned. I gave him a lift to Hyde Park Corner.'

'Oh, did you?' she said sharply. 'Where did you meet him?'

'At the corner of Lennard Street.'

'I expect he'd been to the shop. Thank heavens I wasn't there to listen to all the boring details of how the publicity over Cordwell is ruining *his* business. He never thinks how harassed *I* am!'

I said casually: 'It seems Trueman had been to see him, to question him about Ericson.'

'I'm getting a bit tired of that name,' she murmured.

'Fairlee said they'd questioned Vivien Gilmore about him,' I went on, watching her closely. 'Has she ever mentioned the name to you?'

'Only when she was telling me that Trueman had been asking her if she knew him.' Her forehead furrowed. 'Tim, you don't think Vivien does know this man Ericson?'

I smiled ironically. 'If she does, she's hardly likely to confide in me.'

She couldn't repress a little smile. 'It was silly of me to say that. But in this atmosphere of suspicion one begins to doubt even one's friends.' She slid a finger across the table towards me, then abruptly withdrew it. 'You're not suspicious of *me*, are you, Tim?'

'Of course not. Why should I be?'

She didn't answer, but glanced at her wristwatch. 'Now I really must go.' Gathering her gloves and handbag, she got up. 'I hate leaving you like this, but . . .'

I stood up. 'You can't manage dinner, later?'

'I'm afraid not. I'll be at Vivien's flat until all hours.' She rested a hand on my arm. 'But if anything should occur to you about why my flat was searched, do ring me at Vivien's. You'll find her number in the book.'

I promised her I would, and accompanied her to the door.

She disappeared into the busy traffic of Park Lane, and I returned to the bar.

I beckoned the waiter over, ordered another sherry, and sat gathering my thoughts. It was when I took out my cigarette case again and was tapping on it reflectively that things suddenly began to add up. Barbara's flat must have been broken into by the same two men who had searched mine; they were obviously looking for what they'd failed to find in my flat . . . Something that could have been hidden in a doll.

I was wearing the same suit that I'd worn on the night of the murder. I felt in the ticket pocket of my jacket, and my fingers found what they wanted . . . the key of Barbara's flat . . .

4

Closing the front door, I stood for a moment in the darkness of the hallway at 23 Crawford House Mansions, listening. I was remembering Richards' words: 'But you can take care of yourself, can't you, Frazer? . . . A lot of other people have said the same thing . . . Perhaps Leo Salinger said it . . .' It was a risk I had to take.

I crossed to the living room door and pushed it wide with a gloved hand. I wasn't going to be caught a second time if

Trueman should have any reason to look for fingerprints again. The room was in darkness, the heavy curtains already drawn across the window. In the light from my pocket torch the chairs and settee yawned at me vacantly.

I went quickly to the bedroom and eased the door open. An empty, pink-coverletted bed; a wardrobe with its door ajar; two feathered mules nestling like love-birds on the floor; the faint, elusive fragrance of Barbara's perfume. That was all.

I went back into the living room, and switched on the light. Then, suddenly, my mind clarified. I would try to reenact the scene when Cordwell had faced his murderer.

All my reasoning was based on two assumptions; that the aroma of the cigar smoke I'd noticed in the room on the night of the murder had more than casual significance; and that Cordwell's immediate reaction to an attack had passed unnoticed by his murderer. Also, I was gambling on the chance that the previous searchers hadn't followed my own line of reasoning, in which case it was unlikely they would have found what I was looking for.

I went over to the spot where Cordwell's body had lain, took a cigarette from my case, and put it in my mouth. Then I turned towards the door, imagining I'd suddenly realised the imminence of an attack, and acted in the instinctive manner of a man about to grapple with an assailant. I tore the cigarette from my mouth and flung it from me; and only then did I take my eyes from my imaginary adversary.

My cigarette had fallen beside a waste-paper basket. I picked up the cigarette, then examined the contents of the waste-basket.

Torn envelopes and circulars were not what I was looking for, but there was nothing else. I did some weights and measures calculations. What Cordwell had snatched from his lips would have carried twice the distance of a flimsy cigarette. Accordingly, I widened the radius of my search and presently came to the fireplace.

My hands were trembling as I knelt down and fumbled under the iron legs of an electric fire on the hearth. Then my fingers touched a smooth, cylindrical object. I drew it out and stood up. In my hand I held a half smoked cigar in a chunky holder. It was the holder I had last seen clamped between Cordwell's teeth at the *Café De Kroon*.

I crossed to a table, took out my breast pocket handkerchief, spread this out, and put the cigar and holder on it. Using a paper-knife which was lying on the table, I cut open the cigar. There was a pungent smell of stale tobacco. I shredded the leaf between my fingers, then picked up the cigar-holder, and examined it closely. It was meerschaum, heavily stained with nicotine, about two inches long. I'd been holding it gingerly between finger and thumb, not much relishing its intimate association with the dead Cordwell, when I spotted a groove between the mouthpiece and cup. Using the thumbs and fingers of both hands this time, I unscrewed the mouthpiece. Taking a match from my pocket I prodded the obstruction in the cup of the holder . . .

Two fair-sized stones, sparkling prismatically, fell into the palm of my hand . . .

CHAPTER EIGHTEEN

I

'They're diamonds, all right. I can't value them off-hand, but you can take it from me, they're worth a packet, Frazer!'

It was the afternoon of the day following my discovery of the diamonds in Barbara's flat. I'd tried all morning to contact Ross, but neither he nor Richards had been available. Now I was in the library at Smith Square, watching Richards sliding the diamonds along Ross's blotter with a long, bony finger.

'Richards was once in the diamond business,' Ross said dryly. He turned to me. 'This all ties in with certain facts we've managed to dig up. Interpol's dossier on Cordwell shows a past record of convictions on the Continent for dealing in stolen gems. In my opinion, Cordwell was acting as a courier for Ericson, smuggling diamonds into this country. He also has a record as a blackmailer.'

I smiled. 'Yes, I picked up that bit of information myself – from Barbara Day. Trueman told her about Cordwell. I think he was trying to find out whether she was being blackmailed by him.'

'It's a motive for murder,' Ross said. 'But not in this instance. Cordwell was killed because someone knew he had these diamonds on him.'

'And Ericson had arranged to meet Cordwell in Barbara Day's flat,' Richards interjected. 'That sticks out a mile.'

'Which makes her one of the members of this diamond smuggling organisation,' I said, frowning. 'I just don't believe it! Remember I was watching her when she came into the flat and found Cordwell's body. She was completely surprised, and obviously horrified. In fact she was in an absolute panic when she phoned the police.' I shook my head. 'She's as bewildered as the rest of us.'

Ross waved a restraining hand as Richards leaned forward in his chair. 'But remember that earlier phone call from Vivien Gilmore. Does Barbara Day still deny she's ever heard of Ericson?'

'She asked me today whether I thought Vivien Gilmore knew Ericson. In a way that might explain the phone call. Suppose Vivien does know Ericson – is having an affair with him without realising he was mixed up in anything like this. Wouldn't that explain Miss Day's denial of Ericson – one woman protecting another?'

'It's ingenious, but it doesn't account for Cordwell being found dead in Barbara Day's flat.'

'No,' I agreed. 'It doesn't.'

Ross had been drumming his fingers on the desk, inattentively, during this conjecture. Now he pursued another line of thought: 'You say you thought you recognised the barrow boy as one of the men who raided your flat?'

'I'm practically positive of it.'

'Are you suggesting they also broke into Miss Day's flat?'

'Well, someone did – we can only assume it was the same two who raided mine.'

Ross nodded. 'How I see it is this: if they were in Ericson's organisation, then you suggest they got wind of his meeting with Cordwell, double-crossed Ericson, and murdered Cordwell to get the diamonds for themselves?'

Richards fixed his eyes on the ceiling. 'Of course, one of the men could be Ericson himself. Perhaps he lost his temper with Cordwell,' he suggested.

'It's possible, I grant you, Richards.' Ross rubbed his chin thoughtfully for a moment, then waved his hand in the direction of the three metronomes which were now standing on his desk. 'We've had these examined. They're perfectly ordinary metronomes. Just what their significance is escapes me at the moment. Any ideas, Frazer?'

'It's obvious that Dempsey is in the Ericson organisation,' I said tentatively. 'He could be a fence, using his business as a cover for the buying of stolen diamonds. The bulb catalogue is a passport, as it were, to identify the seller. As an additional precaution the thief must also give the code words – in this instance, "Fantasy, two-thirty".' I leaned forward. 'But there is a third procedure to be gone through – a procedure in some way connected with a metronome.'

'Did this fellow Dempsey say anything when he produced the metronome?' asked Ross.

'Nothing at all. It seemed to be my cue to talk. I was damned relieved when his telephone rang.'

'You said the voice on the telephone sounded familiar to you?' Richards said.

'I'm practically sure it was Vivien Gilmore's,' I said. 'If so, then that puts her in the Ericson organisation. And Dempsey will have enlightened her about you.' Ross's eyes met mine. 'From now on you can expect trouble, Frazer.'

'And not only from Ericson's outfit,' Richards commented quietly. 'Trueman hasn't finished with you yet, my boy. From what you've told me, he's still far from convinced that you didn't keep that appointment with Barbara Day on the night Cordwell was murdered.'

I looked over at Ross. 'Why don't I take Trueman into my confidence, sir?'

Ross shook his head emphatically. 'Get this quite clear, Frazer. All I'm interested in is Salinger. I want to be sure that he was a reputable agent and not mixed up in this diamond smuggling. The murder is police business. You'll have to talk your way out of that as best you can.' His eyes hardened. 'Once the police know what you're doing the newspapers may get hold of it. Then this department will be in the limelight.' He sniffed contemptuously. 'The sensational press would have a bean feast! "British Secret Agent involved in Cordwell Murder" – all that kind of stuff. There could even be questions in the House . . . No, Frazer, you must handle this case entirely on your own.'

'All right, sir. I understand,' I said. 'But if I'm on my own I must be given a free hand to handle the case in my own way.'

Ross looked at me sharply. 'What do you have in mind, Frazer?'

'I haven't worked out all the details yet,' I said airily. 'But I think a return visit to Dempsey is indicated.'

2

Back in my flat I felt a good deal less confident than I must have appeared to Ross. That I had to see Dempsey again was certain, for he was the obvious link in the chain that might lead me to Ericson; and in order to get at the truth about Leo Salinger my best bet was to force a showdown with the top man in the diamond smuggling organisation. What Ericson's reaction would be in such a situation I had no idea; except that it would probably be highly unpleasant. My concern at the moment was to concoct a story that would persuade Dempsey to pass me on to Ericson. It would have to be a convincing one.

After pacing the carpet aimlessly for half an hour I gave up.

It was well after six o'clock and the light was fading. I switched on the table lamp, and as I did so my heart missed a beat. Had I turned off the light in Barbara's flat last night? I had a nasty feeling I hadn't done so, in my excitement at finding the diamonds.

I decided to phone her. She would be almost certain to mention it if she'd found the light on when she got back the night before. I thumbed through the telephone directory to find the number of the antique shop, trying as I did so to think of a pretext for ringing her. I smiled a little guiltily as I dialled the number. If Richards had been there he'd have certainly made a caustic comment.

Vivien Gilmore answered the telephone. I told her who I was and asked to speak to Barbara. Without replying I heard her call: 'It's the Frazer man, Barbara.'

The receiver changed hands almost immediately and I heard Barbara speaking, almost in a whisper. 'Tim . . . I was just about to go out and ring you.'

So the light must have been on, I thought! 'Anything important, Barbara?' I said aloud.

'Well, yes.' She went on in rapid, low tones: 'I can't tell you now. Could you meet me this evening?'

'How about dinner tonight?'

She hesitated. 'Can you make it somewhere quiet, where we can talk?'

'Meet me at *Marino's* . . . You know it? . . . It's in Charlotte Street . . . I'll be there at seven-thirty.'

We said good-bye and I hung up. As I did so I noticed that the address pad which I always kept beside the telephone had disappeared. It was a leather-covered pad with an alphabetical thumb index. I hadn't had occasion to use it for a couple of days, so I couldn't estimate exactly how long it had been missing. I wondered if the man I'd caught searching my bureau had slipped it into his pocket, intending to check up on my telephone list later. I recalled that the last number I'd jotted down was Barbara's. That would account for her flat having been searched. Otherwise the names and addresses would be of no interest. Fortunately, Ross's was not among them.

Then the telephone rang. Picking up the receiver, I gave my number and heard the click of Button A being pressed; then a precise voice said. 'I am speaking to Mr. Frazer?'

I gripped the receiver as I recognised the voice. It was undoubtedly the man who had slipped the note into my cigarette case. 'Yes,' I said.

'My name is Van Dakar,' the precise voice continued. 'You do not know me.'

'Fantasy in the two-thirty – best tip of the week, guv!' I said, mimicking his barrow boy impersonation. Then: 'I must compliment you on your Cockney accent, Mr. Van Dakar.'

He laughed. 'I have picked it up in your London pubs.' His tone changed. 'You have given your card to my barrow boy friend. You wish to see me, perhaps?'

'Very much,' I said, tenderly fingering the back of my head. 'I still have a painful recollection of our first meeting.'

'You have guessed it was me? It is as well. I can now apologise to you. We made a serious mistake about you, Mr. Frazer.'

'We?' I queried.

'I cannot explain the situation over the telephone. But when I do so you will realise that I and my companion had a legitimate reason for searching your flat.'

'And for stealing my telephone pad?' I suggested.

'I do not understand you, Mr. Frazer. Nothing was taken from your flat by us.' His tone became thoughtful. 'Yes . . .

I think it is very important that we meet as soon as possible. At once, perhaps?'

'I'm afraid I can't manage that. I've a dinner date for seven-thirty.'

'Ah! Where is this dinner date, please?'

I hesitated. But there was an urgency in his tone which suggested I'd be satisfying more than curiosity by meeting him that night. 'Charlotte Street,' I answered. 'I'm dining there.'

'And the number of your car?' I shrugged. '297 GPD.'

'When you leave your friend after dinner you will drive, please, to Grosvenor Square and stop just before you come to the main door of the American Embassy,' he instructed in businesslike tones. 'I will be on the kerb there at eleven o'clock.'

'Why all the cloak and dagger stuff?' I asked irritably. 'Why can't we meet for a drink somewhere?'

'It is better that we are not seen together,' he said gravely. 'I must warn you, Mr. Frazer, these people that we are concerned with will not hesitate at violence – or worse.'

That 'we' again. 'I'd feel more comfortable if I knew who you were, Mr. Van Dakar,' I said sharply.

'I will set your mind at rest later, after you have dined with Miss Day.'

'Just a minute!' I exclaimed. 'I didn't say . . .'

'It was a shot in the dark, Mr. Frazer,' he interrupted with a short laugh. 'It is as well that you are not dining with Miss Day in her flat. Now you will be able to enjoy your coffee with peace of mind.'

'What the devil are you getting at?' I demanded heatedly.

Then I heard a gasp and the sound of splintering glass, and the clatter of the receiver falling to the shelf of the call-box.

'Van Dakar!' I called out. 'Van Dakar – what's happened?'

There was a strange choking sound and then a jumble of voices and a woman's scream. I kept calling, 'Hello,' but there was no answer, and finally someone slammed down the receiver at the other end.

I replaced my receiver and hesitated. It would be impossible to trace the call. Perhaps the police should be notified?

Eventually I decided to take no action, as putting through a 999 call would involve me in explanations of more than passing interest to the police. I didn't want Trueman to start questioning me again.

In any case, I was at a loss for an explanation of Van Dakar. From the little he had told me I had the impression that he was on the Law and Order side of the fence. And from the noises in the call-box it seemed highly unlikely that he would be keeping our appointment at eleven. I glanced at my watch. I had twenty minutes to get to Charlotte Street.

3

Marino's is a favourite restaurant of mine; so I was automatically given a corner table. The head waiter brought me a Tio Pepe and handed me a menu. I tried to divert my mind from Van

Dakar by selecting the dishes I would recommend to Barbara. I was still rather on edge from the episode of the call-box and I didn't want her to notice it. I was expecting to have to do some clever fencing, anyway, about the light being on in her living room the previous night; I'd had the distinct impression that she'd suspected me at first of being connected with the searching of her flat that afternoon.

Directly I saw her I knew that whatever else was scheduled for the evening it was not dinner with me. She wore her red suit and a mere wisp of a hat.

'I'm terribly sorry,' she said contritely, 'but I'm afraid our dinner date's off.'

I experienced a sense of relief, which I did my best to conceal. I rose, and drew out a chair. 'At least you can spare time for a drink,' I said. 'You look as though you need a tranquilliser.'

'I do, indeed,' she sighed, sitting down. 'But I've no time. Vivien's waiting in my car. There's a hitch over a drum-top table we bought at St. Albans. We have a customer for it, and now the auctioneer says he didn't accept our bid. Vivien can't wait to have it out with him.'

I thought it rather a late hour for a business row with an auctioneer, and said so.

'He does a lot of deals in his local at night,' Barbara said indifferently, then toyed with the cutlery in front of her. 'But I simply had to see you, Tim. It's about my flat. Another very odd thing has happened.'

'Oh?' I said, noncommittally.

'I have two keys to my flat. One I keep here' – she tapped her handbag – 'the other is always in the Chinese dish on my hall table.'

To bridge the pause, which I felt to be a little too obviously pointed, I said: 'Go on . . .'

'When I looked for the spare key this morning it had disappeared! I tried to phone you at once, but there was no reply.'

'Why did you phone me, Barbara? There's nothing I could do about it.'

'Of course not, I know that, but . . .' Her eyes rebuked me. 'Well, you knew about my flat having been searched, and I thought you'd show some interest in the disappearance of my key.'

I tried to show some interest in a key which was at that moment in a pocket of a suit in my wardrobe. 'If that key was used to get into your flat, how would the – er – visitor have got hold of it?' I asked her.

'That's what bothers me.' She met my eyes for a long moment. 'Someone who visited my flat in the last few days must have taken it.'

I waited for her to go on.

'There have only been four people,' she continued, watching me. 'Vivien, Arthur, that detective . . . and you.'

'You're forgetting Cordwell,' I put in quickly. 'And his murderer.'

'Cordwell was murdered—' she began; then in a startled voice: 'The murderer! Did he take the key . . . and come back yesterday?'

It was a problem that I thought I'd solved until I'd had that phone call from Van Dakar. Now I'd readjusted my thinking. 'It's possible,' I said, then threw the really loaded question at her. 'How did Cordwell get into your flat in the first place?'

She stared at me for a second, then said quietly: 'You're not suggesting that I gave him one of my keys?'

I said weakly: 'No, what I meant – but expressed it very clumsily – was that the murderer could have entered your flat by the fire-escape, and then when Cordwell rang the door bell . . .'

'Oh, Tim,' she said wearily, 'why would Cordwell be calling on me?'

'He was staying in London. He could have looked you up in the phone book, decided to drop in on you . . .'

She stood up. 'Isn't it the same old circle? It simply doesn't lead anywhere.' She glanced at her watch. 'Heavens, I've been here ten minutes – Vivien will be having a fit.' Her eyes softened. 'I feel an absolute beast walking out on you like this.'

'There's always another night,' I suggested. 'Tomorrow perhaps?'

'I'm dining with Arthur tomorrow night. And every other night this week I have engagements.' Suddenly her face brightened. 'I know! I'll make sure we're back from St. Albans by ten. Drop in at my flat just after. We'll have coffee together.'

At that moment the patron himself came to the table, spreading his hands in consternation at her obviously imminent departure. She smiled winningly at him, and with a wave of her hand she was gone.

I reassured the patron, who was protesting that he was coming to take Madame's order personally. 'It wasn't the service,' I assured him. 'Her sister's ill.'

I ordered the scampi, which merited his recommendation. But my mind was more concerned with the coffee which was to follow . . . the coffee at ten, in Barbara's flat.

4

After leaving the restaurant I found myself in an unsettled frame of mind, a mixture of frustration at Barbara Day's evasion, and anticipation of our next meeting. I sat in my car for some minutes, wondering how to spend the next hour or so. There were plenty of inviting pubs within easy reach, but I felt that it was important to keep a clear head.

In the end I decided that I might as well go back to my flat, just in case there should be any telephone calls before ten. I started the engine and drove slowly to the top of Charlotte Street. As I turned right, with a careful eye on my driving mirror for any following traffic, I caught sight of a black saloon car drawing out from the kerb by *Schultz's*. It swung round the corner close behind me. In Tottenham Court Road I had to pull up for the traffic lights at Oxford Street and saw the black saloon swerve sharply in towards the Dominion Cinema, as if bound for Holborn.

A couple of minutes later, however, it was only twenty yards behind me in Oxford Street. I took advantage of the traffic flow to turn quickly down a narrow side street on my left, and when I saw the black saloon in my mirror once more, I knew I was being trailed.

As I steered carefully down the narrow Soho street my brain whirled with speculations as to the identity of my pursuer. I tried several times to get a glimpse of the driver of the car through my mirror, but the angles seemed to be all wrong. All I could see were reflections on the windscreen.

Turning right into Shaftesbury Avenue I made the most of a clear stretch of road and passed through one set of traffic lights on red, leaving my pursuer to wait for the next change to green.

In the swirl of the thick traffic in Piccadilly Circus I thought I'd lost the black saloon, but as I passed Green Park it was visible in my driving mirror again. I thought of Van Dakar's warning: 'These people will not hesitate at violence – or worse.'

The black saloon kept a steady twenty yards behind me as we negotiated the crazy roundabout at Hyde Park Corner and headed for Knightsbridge. I tried to figure out why they should be following me. If they'd planned some sort of attack, surely it would have been easier to wait for me in the dimly-lit mews. Or didn't they know where I lived?

I glanced at the petrol gauge; there was enough in the tank to keep me going if I just drove around until I was due to meet Barbara again. But that would only have meant being followed to her flat. I decided that I had to shake off the black saloon once and for all.

Just past Brompton Oratory I took the left fork, and at the

end of Beauchamp Place I pulled up quickly, jumped out of the car, and dodged past the bus queue, into the station arcade. I ran almost to the end, then turned into the opening to the Piccadilly Line. The lift was ascending with infuriating deliberation, and I lost patience. I darted down the steps to the Inner Circle Line just as a westbound train was coming in. I muttered something to the ticket collector, then rushed down the steps, three at a time. As I shot into the train the doors began to close, as if on cue. Breathless, I sank into a seat, satisfied that no one could have followed me on to that train.

Leaving the train at Gloucester Road I gave the ticket collector a shilling and went out into the street. I still regarded every black saloon suspiciously, but their drivers never glanced my way. When I came to my mews I walked round to the back entrance from the square.

I entered the flat as quietly as possible, carefully closing the door after me and putting up the catch. I flung open the living room door and waited a second before entering. I looked behind the door, then crossed to the window and drew the curtains before switching on the light. The room seemed unnaturally quiet.

When I was halfway through a cigarette I felt much more relaxed. The clock in the corner chimed nine. I blew out a long stream of smoke and decided I'd go back to Beauchamp Place to pick up the car.

Leaning back in my armchair I tried to work out what plans Barbara Day had for me at our meeting, but the heavy silence of the flat was beginning to be unnerving. I reached over to switch on my transistor, but before I could do so the door bell rang.

In my haste to switch off the light I nearly knocked over the radio. Four more strides took me over to the window, where I peeped cautiously through the curtains. There in the mews below was the familiar black saloon car.

The door bell rang again.

I decided that the showdown might as well come now as later; at least I was on my home ground and fully alert. I switched on the light again and went to the front door. My plan was to open it quietly for a few inches and stand prepared to slam it into the intruder's face.

'It's all right, sir – nothing to fear,' said a familiar voice as the door opened. I pulled it wider and immediately recognised the man in the raincoat and grey homburg. It was Detective-Inspector Trueman.

5

I stepped back a pace, my hand on the catch.

'Good evening, sir. Is it convenient for me to come in?' Trueman said, one eyebrow raised in a sort of amused quirk.

'Of course,' I said shortly. 'Why shouldn't it be?'

He came in, taking off his hat. 'I thought perhaps, sir, you might have a visitor already.'

'This isn't my night for feminine company.' I grinned at him. 'Pity she had to miss the scampi at *Marino's*. It was excellent. How was the food at *Schultz's*, Inspector?'

'I can recommend the soups, sir,' he replied imperturbably.

'Sorry I had to keep you waiting so long,' I said. 'Why didn't you come straight here, instead of playing cops and robbers? Rather melodramatic, following me like that, wasn't it?'

'I didn't want to miss you, Mr. Frazer. You might have had another appointment.'

'Well, I hadn't. And what made you trail Miss Day to *Marino's*?'

'Routine, sir. A body was found in her flat in unexplained circumstances; checking on her movements is all part of our routine inquiries.'

'You mean you hope she might lead you to the murderer? Somewhat naive, isn't it, Inspector?'

'To think that the murderer may have been a friend of hers, Mr. Frazer?' He gave me a derisive glance. 'How would he have got into Miss Day's flat if she hadn't known him?'

'By the fire-escape,' I said simply. 'I remember you taking a look at it the morning after the murder.'

He smiled thinly. 'Yes. As a matter of fact, we finger-printed it.'

I tried to remember whether I'd touched the balustrade as I ran down the steps. Trueman's eyes were probing my face. To evade them I turned to the drinks table. 'What will you have, Inspector?'

'Not for me, thank you, Mr. Frazer.'

'Never drink on duty, eh, Inspector?'

'That's right, sir.' He twisted his hat round in his hands.

'Well, if you don't mind . . . ?' I said, picking up my brandy glass.

'There are one or two questions I'd like to clear up with you, Mr. Frazer.'

'Oh . . .' I said; then, with a laugh which I hoped didn't sound as hollow to him as it did to me: 'Is it against the rules to sit down on duty?'

He sat down, and I straddled a high-backed chair, facing him. I had an idea that if the questions became awkward I could get up and pace the room without making it look too obvious.

'Well, what's the first question?' I said easily.

'It concerns your movements on the night of the murder, sir. I think I remember your saying you were unable to keep your appointment with Miss Day.'

I nodded. 'I'd gone down to Slough and couldn't get back in time.'

'I see.' He closed one eye speculatively. 'What was the purpose of your visit to Slough, sir?'

I'd already planted a plausible story in Barbara's mind. Now once again I went into my piece about my business troubles; having gone down to Slough looking for a job; then ducking the issue.

'I know how you felt, sir.' He nodded sympathetically when I'd finished, then looked thoughtful. 'It makes it rather awkward though, Mr. Frazer.' He smiled bleakly. 'I mean, there's no one with whom we can check that you were in Slough at seven-thirty on the night of the murder.'

'You think I'm lying?' I said heatedly.

His eyes travelled across my face almost abstractedly. Without any change of expression he murmured casually: 'You've never been in the diamond trade, have you, Mr. Frazer?'

'The diamond trade! Of course I haven't. I told you – I'm an engineer.' I rose from the chair and began the room-pacing act. 'What's behind that question, Inspector?'

'Routine, sir,' he replied coolly. 'I thought perhaps that might have been what brought you and Cordwell together in Amsterdam. A sort of common interest in diamonds.'

'Let's get this quite clear, Inspector,' I said irritably. 'I met Cordwell *once*. With Miss Day. I can't even remember what we talked about – but it certainly wasn't diamonds.'

He flicked a non-existent speck of dust from his hat. 'Then it will come as a surprise to you to know that Cordwell dealt in stolen diamonds.'

I tried to register the appropriate surprise. 'But it's un-believable! He looked and behaved like any other American tourist.' I turned, and paced behind Trueman's chair, trying to fathom what he was leading up to. At last I said: 'I'm afraid I'm not quite following the drift of all this, Inspector.'

'I was coming to that, sir. In view of what we now know about Cordwell it is fairly certain that whoever murdered him was after the diamonds he was carrying.'

'You know that he was carrying diamonds at the time?' I asked innocently.

'He was in the habit of smuggling them into this country from the Continent. It's likely that he had some with him that evening.' Trueman turned in his chair, facing me. 'Possibly they were hidden in that doll, Mr. Frazer.' I looked blank. 'Doll? What doll?'

'There was a doll in the room by the body. It was ripped open.'

I snapped my fingers. 'I remember now! He'd bought a souvenir doll in Amsterdam; a man in national costume, on a bicycle.'

'That's the one, Mr. Frazer,' Trueman said, nodding. 'And you never saw it again after that meeting in Amsterdam?'

'How could I? I never saw Cordwell again.'

'You're positive about that, sir? You never saw him again, alive' – he paused heavily – 'or dead?'

'What the hell are you getting at?' I demanded furiously, coming round and glaring down at him.

'Your fingerprints, Mr. Frazer. We found them on the door of Miss Day's living room.'

I laughed. 'Of course you did! I was in there the next day.' I finished my brandy. 'And, incidentally, Inspector, how do you know they *were* mine?'

He put a hand in his pocket. 'We checked from this, sir,' he said slowly, holding out my telephone pad.

Staring at it, I said lamely: 'So you stole it that morning you were here?'

'I took that liberty, sir. Although "stole" is not the word. "Appropriated in the course of police inquiries" is a more accurate description.'

'Call it what you like!' I snapped. 'All right, you found the fingerprints I made the following day. What's the significance of that?'

'There wouldn't be any significance, sir,' he said coldly, 'except that your fingerprints were among those we took *on the night of the murder* . . .' His eyes hardened. 'Would you care to explain how they got there, Mr. Frazer?'

My door bell rang. It seemed that I was fated to be saved by the bell from answering awkward questions. Trueman rose, with every intention, it appeared, of answering the door himself.

'Don't bother, Inspector,' I said, crossing to the door. 'It may not be a man with a gun.'

It was Richards. Glimpsing Trueman across my shoulder his face froze. 'If you're busy, Frazer . . .'

I almost dragged him in by the lapels. 'Inspector Trueman was just leaving, weren't you, Inspector?' I said.

Somewhat reluctantly Trueman moved to the door. 'Yes, sir. But I shall be wanting to talk to you again very shortly,' he said curtly.

'I'll look forward to that,' I replied. 'By the way, this is Lewis Richards . . . Inspector Trueman.'

For a second, as they nodded a greeting, I thought I caught a look of bewilderment flash across the Inspector's face when he heard the name. Then he was saying: 'Perhaps you'd telephone me, Mr. Frazer, should an explanation of the matter we've been discussing occur to you.'

'I'm sure there is one, Inspector.'

He smiled wryly. 'I hope so, sir. Good night.'

'Trouble?' inquired Richards, when the Inspector had gone.

'Plenty. I left my fingerprints on the inside door of Barbara Day's flat.'

'What of it? He knows you've been there.'

'But not *before* the police found Cordwell's body.'

'I still don't get it. How could he check that they were your fingerprints?' He cocked his head at me. 'You haven't a police record, have you, old boy?'

'It seems I'm getting one. Trueman helped himself to my telephone pad when he was here before.' I glanced over to where he had been sitting. 'And, damn him, he's gone off with it again!'

Richards whistled soundlessly. 'You've got yourself in a nasty jam, Frazer. Why in hell weren't you more careful?'

'I didn't know I was going to find a body,' I said testily. 'Anyway, what brings you here?'

Richards took a rolled sheet of paper from his inside pocket. 'I'd like you to take a look at this.'

When I'd unrolled it I saw that it was a flashlight photograph of a man's head, propped up on pillows. His eyes were closed and his mouth hung open. He was either dead, or very near it.

'Who is it?' I asked quietly.

'A man called Van Dakar. He's a Dutchman.'

I looked, with some apprehension, more closely at the photograph, trying to associate the face with the smiling barrow boy. It was the shape of the head, the fair hair, and the prominent cheekbones which eventually convinced me. 'Yes, I recognise him. It's the man who gave me the tip from a barrow in Lennard Street.'

'That's where he was shot. In Lennard Street. While he was phoning from a call-box.'

'He was phoning me!' I said quickly. 'I knew something had happened to him at the time.' I glanced again at the photograph. 'But I didn't imagine it was anything like this.'

'That photograph was taken in hospital twenty minutes ago. He hasn't recovered consciousness, and I doubt whether he ever will.' Richards tapped his chest, just above the heart. 'He was hit here.'

'Who shot him? Have they got the man?'

Richards shook his head. 'He was shot from a passing car; it got clear away.'

I handed the photograph back to Richards. 'How did you come by this?' I inquired.

'I'm still on this case, you know, Frazer,' he replied cagily. 'Tell me about this phone call.'

I did my best to recount every detail of the telephone call from Van Dakar.

'So he gave you a warning.' Richards smiled grimly. 'Ironic, isn't it, that a moment later it was he who was shot?'

'But why was he shot? And by whom?' My spine tingled as I realised these were questions to which we would have to find the answer very soon.

'Didn't he give you any clue as to his identity?'

'None. Though I had the impression that he could have

been working for some department such as ours. He wasn't one of Ross's men, was he?'

Richards shook his head. 'He could have been in the Dutch undercover police, possibly tracing stolen diamonds. Equally, he could have been in the diamond smuggling game himself. I don't suppose Ericson has cornered the entire market in stolen diamonds.'

I frowned. 'But why should Van Dakar warn me that I was in danger? And give me that tip?'

Richards shrugged. 'Maybe that was just to see what you'd do.'

Suddenly I remembered Van Dakar's reference to coffee with Barbara Day. 'Here's a darned odd thing,' I said. 'Van Dakar guessed I was having dinner with Barbara tonight . . .'

'His guess seems to have been as good as mine,' Richards murmured.

Ignoring this remark I went on: 'But the point is, when he heard we were dining at a restaurant and not at Barbara's flat he said: "Then you will be able to enjoy your coffee with peace of mind".'

'M'm . . . Cryptic, to say the least.' Richards paused. 'Did you enjoy your coffee?'

'Barbara had to call the date off – for business reasons,' I said. 'But she *has* asked me to go to her flat tonight for coffee.'

He grinned at me as he helped himself to a cigarette. 'As I said once before, you can take care of yourself, Frazer. And, talking of that, what about this return visit to the bulb importer?'

'That's already scheduled,' I said carelessly. 'But I'll want one or two things from you first. Sit down, Richards, and I'll tell you what they are.'

6

As I followed Barbara into the living room of her flat I was mystified yet again that such an attractive woman should be satisfied with a neurotic hypochondriac like Fairlee. With her looks and figure she could have looked much further than the Stock Exchange for her life partner.

In the living room she turned to me with a swift, engaging smile, as though she were welcoming an old friend. 'Make yourself comfortable, Tim.'

She had changed into a black dress, plain except for a simple spray of diamonds.

Barbara walked over to the coffee tray. On it, with the cups, was a glass coffee-percolator, a spirit lamp burning beneath it.

'You don't mind waiting, do you, Tim? I've a thing about making coffee this way.'

I smiled. 'How did the brawl with the auctioneer go?'

'Trust Vivien to handle a situation like that. Of course, there were a lot of fireworks, but eventually he promised to deliver the drum-top table by ten tomorrow.'

'Never a dull moment in the antique business!' I brought out my cigarette case.

'Certainly not in ours! We had a visit from that detective just after you phoned today.'

'Trueman? What's on *his* mind?'

I lit her cigarette and she exhaled slowly before replying: 'You, Tim.'

'You make that sound rather ominous.'

'In a way it is.' She gave a small sigh. 'Why must we always be discussing this wretched Cordwell business?' Her eyes softened. 'There are so many other things I want to talk to you about, Tim.'

'Hadn't you better disperse this cloud that's hanging over my head first?'

'It's about the appointment we had on the night of the murder. Apparently Trueman's not convinced that you didn't turn up.' She smiled remotely. 'It seems that now I'm suspected of loaning the key of my flat to you.'

I waved that idea away with a deprecating flourish of my hand. 'Why should Trueman fling that one at you?'

'He says he's found your fingerprints on my living room door.'

I wasn't ready at that juncture to tell her of Trueman's talk with me. 'Why shouldn't he find my fingerprints in your flat? He saw me here the morning after Cordwell was killed.'

'That's what I pointed out to him.' She looked at me with a puzzled expression. 'Although he didn't actually say it, I felt all the time that he was leading up to something else; that you could have been in my flat the night before.'

'Do you agree with him, Barbara?' I asked quietly.

'Of course not!' she exclaimed, with an impatient gesture. 'How could you have been? You were still at Slough when you phoned me long after seven-thirty that night.'

The telephone rang and, excusing herself, she picked up the receiver. She gave her number, then glanced over at me as the caller identified himself. 'Oh, hello, Arthur . . . Yes, I'm alone . . .' She nodded her head wearily while a voice droned at the other end. 'Have you taken your tablets, Arthur? . . . Well, you must give them time to act, dear.' She listened to a lengthy protest. 'All right then, Arthur – I'll come round. In about half an hour. See you then, dear.'

With a sigh, she replaced the receiver. 'I suppose it *is* another of his asthma attacks. But sometimes I wonder if he doesn't play on my sympathy and make them an excuse to have me run round and fuss over him.'

I put on an expression of polite impartiality. 'One can't help feeling sorry for him, I suppose.'

She nodded, not very enthusiastically, then darted back to the table and blew out the flame beneath the percolator. 'Goodness! I almost forgot the coffee!'

She sat down and began to pour it.

'Do you take sugar, Tim?'

My cigarette had burned down to a stub, scorching my fingers, but I couldn't risk taking my eyes from the coffee just then.

'Two lumps, please.'

'Oh, dear, I was afraid you might. And I've run out of it. Do you mind having saccharine?'

I heard myself saying I didn't mind, then I let my cigarette

stub drop into the ashtray as Barbara produced a small bottle
and dropped two tiny white tablets into my coffee. She handed
me the cup and leaned back in her chair.

'Arthur really *would* have an attack if he knew you were here
having coffee with me.' She gave me an amused glance. 'Vivien
swears he's jealous of you.'

'He's the type who'd be jealous of the milkman,' I said,
laughing. 'By the way, was Vivien there when Trueman dropped
in on you this afternoon?'

She nodded. 'Very much so. I had to listen to her theories
on the Cordwell case all the way to St. Albans and back.'

'Were her theories plausible?'

She bit her lip thoughtfully before answering. 'You know
Vivien can't make you out, either. She wanted to know whether
you ever made a pass at me in Amsterdam. When I said you
certainly didn't, she took the attitude that – well, if he's not
the sort of man who makes passes at engaged girls why is he
running around after you now?' She lowered her voice. 'Why
are you, Tim?'

Once again I was saved by the bell. This time it was the
door bell. She looked at me without speaking, then got up and
went out into the hall. Directly I heard her opening the front
door I changed my coffee cup for hers.

'Vivien!' I heard Barbara exclaim. 'Is anything wrong?'

'Don't panic,' said Vivien's strident voice. 'I left my cigarette
case in your car, that's all.'

Barbara was saying, 'Oh, you could have phoned me,' when
Vivien pushed open the living room door.

Her start of surprise on seeing me was just a shade too obvious. 'You're the last person I expected to find here,' she said, then turned back to Barbara. 'I'm sorry, darling . . . If I'd known, I wouldn't have barged in.'

'That's all right,' Barbara said with a forced smile. '*Did* you leave your cigarette case in my car? I don't remember your using it on the way back.'

'Then I've left it on the bar of that pub in St. Albans. That means it'll be stolen!'

'I expect you'll find it's in the pocket of the coat you were wearing,' Barbara said coolly. 'Now you're here you'll stay and have coffee . . . ?'

'Darling, are you sure I'm not interrupting something?'

'I'll get another cup,' Barbara said.

Vivien gave a tiny shrug and smiled at me. 'Nice to see you,' she said, depositing herself in Barbara's chair. 'Really, I feel it's very naughty of me not to have phoned first.'

'Please don't apologise,' I said. 'I was just going, anyway.'

Barbara brought another cup and saucer. 'And *I* have to go and see Arthur. He's been ringing . . .' She clattered the cup and saucer on the table as the telephone rang again. 'Wouldn't it be just like Arthur to want to know why I haven't dashed over right away?'

'Doesn't he ever let you off the leash, Barbara?' Vivien said, raising her eyebrows. She picked up the full coffee cup in front of her, stirring it mechanically.

Presently, Barbara replaced the receiver and came back to

the table. 'He wants me to go round immediately. But I suppose I can be allowed time to drink my coffee first.' She glanced down at Vivien. 'Oh – you seem to have appropriated it, Vivien.'

'Oh, sorry, darling,' Vivien began. 'I'll pour you another . . .'

I hastily sipped my own. 'Hello!' I exclaimed, watching Barbara's face. 'There seems to have been a mix-up with the cups. This one isn't sweetened.'

'Oh, Tim, you must have got mine,' Barbara said. 'Never mind, I hadn't started it. Help yourself to more saccharine . . .'

'No, don't bother,' I said quickly. 'I must be going, anyway.'

Barbara picked up her handbag. 'Yes, well, so must I. Arthur's so bad tempered.'

As I got up Vivien said firmly. 'You're not going to drag Mr. Frazer off with you, Barbara; I'm relying on him to give me a lift when I've finished my coffee.'

'Oh,' said Barbara, a trifle petulantly. '. . . Well, you might have asked Tim whether he minded.' She smiled at me. 'I'll give you a ring some time tomorrow.'

'See you in the morning, darling,' Vivien said nonchalantly as she helped herself to a cigarette. 'And you can tell Arthur from me that he takes you too much for granted!'

7

'That man!' Vivien said when the front door had closed 'Possessive isn't the word for it!'

'Sick people usually are,' I said.

'I'm always telling her she'll have an invalid on her hands if ever she does marry him. Can't you persuade her not to rush into this marriage with Arthur?'

'Me?' I protested. 'I don't think I've known Barbara sufficiently long to discuss her personal affairs.'

'I suppose not.' She let the smoke drift from her lips. 'Although you've discussed yours with her, I believe.'

'What exactly do you mean?'

'Well, about your business affairs. She tells me your engineering firm ran into financial difficulties.'

'I did mention something about it,' I admitted. 'But I'm rather surprised that Barbara should have broadcast it.'

Vivien laughed. 'Nothing like that, Mr. Frazer – just one girl to another.' She finished her coffee. 'I suppose you'll start it up again directly you get back on your feet?'

'I suppose so,' I said shortly. 'When I can lay my hands on some capital.'

'That's none too easy, I imagine.' She crossed her legs. 'By the way, did Barbara tell you Inspector Trueman went to see her this afternoon?'

'She did mention it.'

'I wasn't really listening, but I couldn't help overhearing some of his questions ... He seemed very interested in that appointment you had with Barbara.'

'On the night of the murder, you mean? I was detained in Slough. I couldn't keep it.'

'And, of course, you couldn't have got into the flat if you had kept it. Barbara was detained by Arthur – as usual.' She flicked the ash from her cigarette on to the carpet. 'You know, this fingerprint system has always fascinated me. Can they really tell the actual day on which the prints were made?'

'I should imagine you know the answer to that one,' I said, with a dry smile. 'What made you say that?'

'It was rather silly of me, wasn't it? Naturally, it would only be the fingerprints found on the night of the murder that would have any significance.' She raised the foot of the crossed leg, and examined the toe of her shoe rather elaborately. 'I heard Trueman telling Barbara that Cordwell was in the stolen diamond racket.'

'He told me that, too,' I said, mentally noting that Barbara hadn't said anything to me about that part of her conversation with Trueman. Had she intended to mention it, I wondered? After all, there'd been some interruptions and it could easily have slipped her mind. Or had she deliberately concealed the information?

'I wonder if he had any diamonds on him the night he was killed?' Vivien was saying. 'If he had, then the murderer must have had quite a haul, mustn't he?'

It was obvious that she was leading up to something, so I decided to play along. 'But could he have done anything with them?' I asked innocently. 'He couldn't just take stolen diamonds into a jeweller's and sell them.'

'There are men who will deal in them. Cordwell must have known one.'

'Then that must be the man he had the appointments with!' I exclaimed, as though suddenly enlightened. 'Ericson! Now I know why Trueman's been questioning me about him.'

'He's questioned us all about him – me, Barbara, Arthur . . .' She laughed lightly. 'Oh, well, if anyone ever comes to me wanting to dispose of stolen diamonds, that's who I'll put them on to – Ericson!'

'If you can find him,' I said, joining in her laugh. 'The police can't.'

'That's true.' She dropped her cigarette stub into the dregs of her coffee. 'So it's no use you finding any stolen diamonds, Mr. Frazer, because you wouldn't be able to get rid of them.' She smiled ruefully. 'What a horrible thought; walking around with the potential capital to start your business up again, and not being able to do a thing about it.'

'Just hunting for a needle in a haystack,' I agreed. 'I wonder what this Ericson looks like.'

'Like any respectable bank manager, I expect.' She stood up. 'I suppose I did rather take it for granted you'd give me a lift. Would you mind, Mr. Frazer?'

'No, of course not,' I said. 'Where can I drop you?'

'Is Sloane Square all right for you?'

'It's on my way,' I told her.

At the front door she paused. 'You know, I think all this trouble has made Barbara see Arthur in a new light. He hasn't shown a scrap of concern for all the worry she's going through.' She arched her eyebrows. 'Your sympathy has meant a great deal to Barbara, Mr. Frazer. She's told me that.'

I mumbled something about a shoulder to cry on.

'Barbara's such a sweet person . . .' She smiled at me meaningly, then tapped my arm with her handbag. 'You must hurry up and get the capital you need to get on your feet again, Mr. Frazer.'

CHAPTER NINETEEN

I

The next morning, as I wandered into the living room, Mrs. Glover was standing by the telephone, duster in hand. As I entered she started to polish the telephone with unnecessary vigour. This, I knew only too well, was a cover for some seemingly innocent probing.

'I meant to ask you, Mr. Frazer,' she began, 'have you put the telephone pad away somewhere?'

I seated myself behind the coffee jug. 'It's in my desk drawer. Did you want it for anything?'

She was slightly taken aback for a moment, but quickly recovered, and started polishing a speckless brass candlestick. 'Did you find out who the lady was that phoned?'

Of course, it had been Barbara; I'd remembered, some time afterwards, that she'd mentioned it when we'd met in the coffee bar. But I wasn't going to enlighten Mrs. Glover on that point. I shook my head and poured myself some coffee.

'There was a police car at the top of the mews this morning when I come in,' she went on persistently. 'I suppose they're keeping an eye on somebody.'

I supposed they were. I was mentally cursing Trueman; my plans for the morning didn't include having fun and games evading a trailing police car. I decided it would be as well to check which end of the mews, in Mrs. Glover's devious mind, was the top.

I adopted her oblique approach. 'Did you notice whether the lilac was out in the square as you came in this morning, Mrs. Glover?'

It no more deceived her than a pill in a piece of meat fools a dog. 'If I was you, Mr. Frazer,' she said, with a flick of the duster, 'I'd use the bottom end of the mews today.' Then the front door bell rang and really made her day. 'Shall I say you're out, sir?' she inquired in an eager whisper.

I overcame my irritation and laughed. 'You're a treasure, Mrs. Glover! Answer the door, then bring another cup and saucer.'

As I'd expected, it was Richards. He came in carrying a small leather case. 'Good morning, Frazer. I've brought what you wanted.'

'Splendid! You'll join me in a coffee, won't you?'

He nodded, smiling. 'Talking of coffee . . .' he began, obviously alluding to my appointment with Barbara the previous evening.

'Forget it!' I said. 'That was a false alarm. I switched the coffee cups.' I then went on to describe what had happened. 'Barbara Day reacted perfectly normally. And Vivien Gilmore certainly showed no sign of being drugged. In fact, her mind was exceptionally active.'

'It sounds as though Van Dakar was just trying to throw a scare into you.'

'Seems like it,' I agreed. 'Though perhaps he doesn't trust Barbara Day any more than you and Ross do.'

Richards pulled his nose. 'And you think she is to be trusted?'

'With one reservation, yes.' I changed the subject quickly. 'By the way, how is Van Dakar?'

'I phoned the hospital this morning. He's recovered consciousness and they think there's a good chance that he'll pull through. I'll have a talk with him this afternoon, if they'll let me.'

Mrs. Glover came in with the extra cup and saucer, eyed Richards covertly, obviously decided he was just a business acquaintance, and retired somewhat disappointed.

I poured Richards a coffee. 'You didn't have any difficulty in persuading Ross to hand over the things I asked for?'

Richards opened the small case on his lap. 'He was a bit sticky about the diamonds.'

'I imagined he might be. But don't worry – I shan't lose them.'

I opened the jewellery box he handed me and examined the two diamonds, which looked very impressive against their black plush background.

Richards delved in the case again. 'And here's the metronome you took from Dempsey.' He put it on the table.

'Just what was I supposed to say when Dempsey produced this?' I rubbed my finger over the polished surface. 'I've a hunch that it's the key to everything we want to know.'

'Which is simply,' Richards said warningly, 'the problem of Leo Salinger. Was he the reputable person Ross thinks he was? Or was he mixed up in the stolen diamond racket? That's all.' He regarded me shrewdly for a moment. 'Don't get too ambitious, Frazer.'

'I'll keep that in mind, Richards,' I replied, not altogether sincerely. I was too deeply involved in a personal way to be satisfied with anything less than the full answers to the side issues that had cropped up in the Leo Salinger case.

'And here's the other thing you wanted.' Richards brought out a small black automatic and balanced it on the palm of one hand. 'Ross looked down his nose when I told him you wanted a loan from the armoury.' He handed it to me, butt first. 'Don't expect the department to give you a medal if you use it.'

I slipped the gun into my jacket pocket. 'For persuasive purposes only,' I explained, with a grin.

Richards smiled back at me, closed the case, and snapped the locks. 'Have you decided what line you'll take with Dempsey?'

'My own special brand of persuasion,' I said.

'Fact – or fiction?'

'Maybe a little of each,' I told him.

2

On my previous visit to Dempsey's office I'd noticed a coffee and sandwich bar a few yards from his building. It was frequented by the porters from Covent Garden when the pubs were closed. Relying on my guess that Dempsey would come out at some time to fill his Thermos flask and purchase sandwiches, I stepped into the doorway of a warehouse facing his office block. I had half an hour's wait; then he came out with his Thermos tucked under one arm.

I watched him go into the coffee bar, then I hurried across the street, into his office building, and swiftly along the dingy passage to his office. If he had locked his door my visit would lose an important asset – the element of surprise. But my luck held. I slid inside the room, and closed the door behind me.

I went over to Dempsey's chair, unwrapped the metronome and placed it in the centre of the desk. Then I reversed the chair, straddled it, took out the gun and laid it beside the metronome, ready to hand.

Presently I heard heavy footsteps coming along the passage. Grunting to himself, Dempsey entered the room and closed the door, apparently preoccupied with the newspaper he was reading.

As he turned it was the metronome which first caught his eye. He froze, staring at it for a moment, then his eyes slowly travelled to the gun I was pointing at him. With a crash the Thermos slipped from his arm to the floor.

'Good morning, Mr. Dempsey,' I said cheerfully. 'Picking a winner for the two-thirty?'

The newspaper slid from his grasp. 'Frazer!' He ran his tongue across his lips. 'What are you doing here?' His voice was hoarse, almost choked.

'Returning your metronome,' I said.

Without taking his eyes from my face he pushed the Thermos flask aside with one foot. 'Why?'

'Our last little talk ended rather abruptly; before we got

around to discussing the metronome.' I smiled. 'I thought it might be a good idea if we had a more friendly chat about it.'

'I see,' he said, glaring at the gun.

'Don't get any wild ideas, Dempsey,' I warned him, making a show of tightening my finger on the trigger. 'Not that I'd shoot to kill – but I can pick my spot at this distance.'

He winced. 'What is it you want?' he gulped at last.

'That's more like it!' I said affably, waving the gun towards the chair in front of the desk. 'Sit down.'

He slumped into the chair and put a packet of sandwiches on the desk. 'Do you mind if I eat a sandwich?' he asked, beginning to tear off the paper.

'Go ahead,' I nodded. 'We'll skip the coffee this morning.'

He looked at me sourly for a moment, obviously recalling the use to which I'd put the scalding coffee at our last meeting; then he pushed the sandwiches across to me with a sudden gesture. 'Corned beef – fresh cut.'

I shook my head. 'Now, Dempsey, about this metronome. You were waiting for me to say something the other day when you produced it, weren't you?'

He picked up a sandwich. 'Was I?' he said cagily. 'Then why didn't you?'

'You didn't give me much time, did you, before pulling a gun on me?'

'You never know who anyone is these days. It might have been a hold-up.' He took a large bite out of the sandwich. 'How did I know you weren't going to stick me up then – like you're doing now, Frazer?'

'Oh, it wasn't my day for carrying a gun. I hadn't any diamonds to protect then.'

He considered this for a few moments as he chewed noisily. 'You have now?' he asked tentatively.

I drew the jeweller's case from my pocket, pressed the catch, and displayed the two stones. Dempsey's eyes bulged.

He wiped the back of his hand across his mouth. 'May I examine them, Mr. Frazer?' He half rose and reached across the desk.

I kept my hand on the case and smacked his arm down with the gun. 'Keep your hands to your side of the desk, Dempsey!'

'Could you pass me my jeweller's eye-glass?' he begged. 'Second drawer down.' I found it and slid it over to him.

He screwed it in his eye and examined the two diamonds expertly. 'What do you want for them?' he asked eventually, taking the glass from his eye.

'Not a middle-man's price. But I'll do a deal with your boss.'

His expression changed. 'Who said I had a boss?'

'Cordwell.'

He brought the half-eaten sandwich to his mouth, then slowly lowered it and replaced it in the packet. 'Are you a friend of Cordwell's?'

'I knew him in America,' I said glibly. 'We were once in business together.'

'What sort of business?'

'We won't go into details,' I replied crisply. 'I lost touch with him for several years. Then I bumped into him a week ago in

Amsterdam. We had a night out.' I shook my head. 'Cordwell never could hold his liquor. He got a bit talkative.'

Dempsey smoothed the sandy hair across his bald pate. 'Talkative about what?'

'His present line of business. Of course, we'd been very closely associated in America, so he didn't hold much back.'

'I always said that bloody big mouth of his meant trouble!' Dempsey scowled down at the diamonds. 'Well, let's have it!'

'He started off by telling me he was smuggling stuff over here from the Continent,' I said, surprised to find how easily the lies rolled out once I'd warmed up. 'After a couple more drinks he really spilled the beans. He said he had a very nice little diamond smuggling racket, and he went on to boast about the size of the organisation he was working for; and the fool-proof code system they used.'

'So that's where you picked it all up,' Dempsey muttered, obviously impressed by my carefully devised story. 'We wondered how you got on to the bulb catalogue and the code words.'

'So you had a Board meeting about me, did you?' I suggested with a laugh. 'Which of the directors were present, besides you and the Chairman?'

'You're not in a bar with a drunk now, Mr. Frazer,' Dempsey said. 'I'm not Cordwell. So don't think you can kid me into dropping names.'

'Well, I'll drop just one name,' I said. 'Ericson. He's the boss of your organisation.'

'Cordwell!' Dempsey spat out the name with contempt.

'The loose-tongued bastard!' He prodded the diamonds with a fleshy finger. 'So now you're onto the set-up and you want us to buy these? We'll have to know where you got them, first.'

'I got them from Cordwell.'

His jaw dropped. 'He sold them to you?'

'No.' I paused, then adopted a confidential tone. 'I'm going to be frank with you, Dempsey. I've an idea that Ericson isn't playing quite square with you.'

'He'd better not try any tricks,' he began angrily; then, more guardedly: 'What do you mean?'

'Have you ever heard of a girl called Barbara Day?' I asked, watching him closely. His stare, as he shook his head, was too mystified not to be genuine, so I continued. 'I met her in Amsterdam. She was on friendly terms with Cordwell. When I returned to London she invited me to her flat for a drink. I went to her flat but no one answered the door bell. Just as I was about to leave . . .' I frowned at him. 'You won't believe this, Dempsey . . .'

'Well, give me the chance,' he said irritably. 'Go on . . .'

'As I was turning away from the door someone slipped a key under it. I picked it up and let myself into the flat. It was empty, except for a body lying on the floor of the living room.'

He moistened his lips. 'Cordwell's?'

I nodded. 'His head was battered in. He'd been murdered. Remembering what he'd told me about being mixed up in the stolen diamond racket I knew his killing must be connected with it. Then I remembered that back in the States he used to smuggle heroin across the Mexican border in a cigar holder. I thought he might be using the same method to smuggle diamonds. His cigar-holder wasn't on him, but just as I was leaving the flat I spotted it lying in the fireplace.' I pointed the gun at the diamonds on Dempsey's desk. 'Those were in the cigar-holder.'

Dempsey breathed heavily, his face flabby and moist with fear. 'You think Ericson . . . ?'

'That's anybody's guess,' I said. 'But if he did, he didn't get the diamonds.'

Dempsey pressed a hand to his stomach. Through an obvious spasm of pain he muttered: 'What's the next move, Frazer?'

'You'll get in touch with Ericson. Tell him I have the diamonds and I'm prepared to do a deal – and no questions asked. I'll be in my flat from seven o'clock tonight.' I reached over, closed the jewel case, picked it up, and put it in my pocket. 'And you might mention also that I haven't as trusting a disposition as Cordwell had.'

I rose and backed to the door. 'I'm sorry to have interrupted your elevenses, Dempsey.'

In the passage, with the door closed behind me, I dropped the gun into my pocket and hurried down to the street.

As I turned up Long Acre, looking for a taxi, a horn honked imperatively and I glanced back to see Richards leaning out of the open door of his car. I went back and opened the far side door.

'The get-away car,' Richards explained, grinning. 'Just in case you had to take a pot at Dempsey and make a dash for it. I expect you need a drink now. We'll go round to the Nag's Head; they should be open by this time.'

3

'Just the place to hear about the events in Dempsey's office,' Richards said, nodding at the pillars plastered with ancient showbills 'It's got the authentic theatrical atmosphere.'

'Everything went according to plan,' I said rather smugly, and went on to tell him all that had happened.

When I'd finished he sipped his sherry thoughtfully. 'A bit risky, letting him know you were in Barbara Day's flat on the night of the murder, wasn't it?'

'You think he might inform the police? And have them digging into his business? Not a chance. I was curious to see what it would stir up, apart from any reaction from Ericson. If I'm right, and it was Vivien Gilmore's voice I heard on Dempsey's telephone, he's certain to pass everything on to her. And it also gave me an opportunity to try out Barbara Day's name on him.'

'Was there any reaction?'

'None. I'm positive he'd never heard her name before.'

'That must have given you a nice, warm glow,' Richards said with a smile. 'Incidentally, what do you intend to do if Ericson does come round to your flat tonight?'

'From the hints I threw out to Dempsey about my adventures with Cordwell in America, Ericson will assume he's dealing with a crook,' I said, doing some quick thinking out loud. 'So I can talk quite freely. My idea is to mention Leo Salinger's name as a man who'd bought stolen diamonds from me. How Ericson reacts to that should definitely either prove that

Salinger was working for Ericson, or confirm Ross's belief in him.'

'It all sounds very simple over a glass of sherry,' Richards said dubiously. 'But you're up against a tough crowd, you know, Frazer.' As though to emphasise his point, he added: 'I've just left one of their victims.'

'Van Dakar? How is he?'

'He has an even chance of pulling through – that is, if there are no complications.'

'You had a talk with him?'

'I was allowed fifteen minutes. He's a private investigator for one of the big Dutch insurance companies. He's been on to this Ericson set-up for some time. Cordwell was known to be smuggling diamonds over for them, and Van Dakar had been trailing him for weeks. He'd followed him to Barbara Day's flat on the night of the murder.'

I smiled grimly. 'He thought I was the murderer, then?'

Richards nodded. 'He also concluded that you had Cordwell's diamonds. Hence the search at your flat.'

'That's understandable. But what beats me is why he should have put that note in my cigarette case to send me to Lennard Street. And why tip me off to the code words?'

'It's that fatal charm of yours, Frazer!' Richards laughed. 'Seriously, when they found no diamonds in your flat, and no evidence there of your being mixed up in that sort of business, they came to the conclusion you were an Interpol man in the stolen gems branch. So, having got no further than Dempsey and come up against a brick wall themselves, they decided to let you in on what information they had, and see what happened.'

'M'm . . . very big of them – though they needn't have been quite so violent,' I said, rubbing the back of my head. 'Did Van Dakar see anyone else that night at Barbara's flat?'

'Nobody. But there's another way out of Crawford House Mansions, across the inner courtyard. So the murderer obviously came down the fire-escape and left that way.'

I sipped my sherry, which reminded me to ask whether Van Dakar had given any explanation of his odd remark about the coffee.

'He said it was meant as a warning that crooks often make use of glamorous women.' He added, slyly: 'Your activities with the cine-camera in Amsterdam didn't go unnoticed.'

'He's definitely not my favourite private eye,' I said shortly. 'Is Barbara Day on his list of suspects?'

'Cordwell stayed at her hotel. she was seen with him in Amsterdam; he went to her flat. It makes an interesting dossier.' Richards glanced at me sharply. 'You're not by any chance falling for her, are you, Frazer?'

'Oh, come off it, Richards! The girl's engaged. And, anyway, apart from the fact that my job is to check up on her, I don't entirely trust her myself since that telephone call of Vivien Gilmore's.'

'And if that had some reasonable explanation?' he persisted.

'I'm always open to conviction,' I grinned at him. 'By the way, how has the avuncular Richards been filling in his spare time? Have you checked up on Fairlee's prospects as a husband-to-be?'

'Not a hope there, Frazer. He's on the Stock Exchange recommended list. His bank manager asks him out to lunch.' He finished his sherry. 'Talking of food, I'll stand you lunch today; a reward for enterprise! They do you very well here.'

4

After lunch I returned to my flat, planning a quiet read and smoke, but I couldn't shake off a feeling of restlessness.

Of course, the seven o'clock meeting with Ericson wasn't exactly something to look forward to with eager anticipation. Supposing he stuck a gun in my stomach directly I opened the door? I patted the revolver in my own pocket. '*Gun Duel in Mews Flat*' would make sensational reading in the morning's newspapers, I reflected. Mrs. Glover would revel in it! That reminded me that she also had a passion for funerals ... My flat felt as cold and lonely as the North face of the Eiger.

Barbara, too, was disturbing me, in more ways than one. Richards had pushed me into a corner with his insistent questioning. True, I hadn't known her long; yet there was a warmth and friendliness in her nature that might, if the circumstances of our meeting had been different, have developed into an intimate relationship.

The front door bell interrupted these thoughts, and I glanced at my watch. It was six o'clock. With my hand on the gun in my pocket, I went to the front door and opened it.

Leaning on his umbrella, wheezing asthmatically, was a

bowler-hatted figure who looked about as frightening as an indignant rabbit. It was Arthur Fairlee.

'There you are, Frazer!' he said, his absurd moustache bristling. 'I must see you on a matter of great importance.'

I took my hand off the butt of the gun, unable to repress an amused smile.

'And I'd prefer to discuss it in private.'

'Come on in then,' I invited, standing back.

He strode past me into the living room, and I followed.

'Sit down and try to relax – or you'll bring on one of your attacks,' I said.

'I would rather remain standing,' he said pompously, planting himself in the middle of the room, his bowler hat pressed to the handle of his umbrella. Then he raised the umbrella and waved it at me. 'I'll come straight to the point; are you having an affair with Barbara?'

'Am I *what*? Now just a minute . . .'

'Are you having an affair with her, Frazer?'

I dodged the ferrule of the umbrella as he advanced a step towards me. The eyes behind the glasses had a near maniacal glare.

'Don't be a bloody fool, Fairlee. Of course I'm not!'

'That's a lie!' he fumed. 'I'm not blind. This hasn't come as a complete surprise to me, Frazer.'

'What hasn't?' I suddenly gripped the revolver in my pocket.

'The breaking of our engagement.'

There was silence for some seconds. Then I heard myself ask. 'When did this happen?'

'Last night – as though you didn't know,' he stammered

excitedly. 'We were perfectly happy until you came on the scene, Frazer.'

'Are you sure, Fairlee? Maybe *you* were. But if Barbara's broken your engagement you've only yourself to blame. You've taken her too much for granted.'

'Only myself to blame!' he exploded. 'Only myself to blame for another man taking advantage of my being ill to steal my fiancée?'

This made me really angry. 'Fairlee, that's not true! On the few occasions we've talked about you, Barbara's been most sympathetic. She'd never listen to any criticism of you, I'm sure of that – she's much too loyal.'

'Breaking off an engagement isn't my idea of loyalty.' He took a further step towards me. 'Do you swear there's nothing between you and Barbara?'

'For God's sake stop dramatising yourself!' I said with irritation. 'Neither Barbara nor I have ever said a word you couldn't have listened to.'

He gave me a long, intense look. 'I accept your word, Frazer,' he said at last. Somewhat reluctantly, he added: 'Perhaps I should apologise.'

I waved his apology aside. 'That's all right – forget it, Fairlee.'

'I wish I could,' he said, self-pityingly. Then, with a sudden change of mood, he went on in an anxious tone: 'Has Barbara ever mentioned the name of any other man to you?'

'In the way I think you mean – no. Of course, she's mentioned various people concerned in this unfortunate business – Cordwell, Trueman...'

'Ericson?' he suggested nervously.

'She denies any knowledge of him,' I said, wondering how much he knew.

'Isn't that significant?' His breath came in short gasps.

'Why should she deny it? I'm certain that she knows him.'

'What makes you think she knows him, Fairlee?'

'I called in at the antique shop yesterday. Vivien was on the telephone. I heard her say: "Ericson wants to meet you again. Shall I fix it for ten tomorrow morning, at *The Dyke*?" Directly Vivien saw me she hung up.'

'How do you know she was speaking to Barbara?' I said sharply.

'Barbara wasn't in the shop. And the guilty way that Vivien cut the conversation short convinced me it was Barbara she was talking to.'

'Did you ask Vivien who it was?'

'Naturally.' He began to pace across the room. 'Of course, she denied it. She said she was talking to a client who wanted her to fix up a meeting with an antique dealer called Merrison. I made a point of dropping in at the coffee bar this morning. Needless to say, neither Vivien nor Barbara put in an appearance.'

'You're positive the name she mentioned was Ericson?'

'No doubt about it.' He blinked at me unhappily. 'Why do they both deny knowing Ericson? Why all this secrecy? I'm positive there's another man behind it. He's responsible for Barbara breaking our engagement. And Vivien is the instigator. She's always disliked me . . .'

I was getting a little tired of this emotional display. 'Why don't you face the facts, Fairlee?' I snapped. 'Barbara broke off the engagement because of your selfishness. But your pride won't let you accept that; you have to pin it on to another man. First it was me – now it's Ericson. And, personally, I think you only imagined it was his name you heard.'

'I hope to God you're right,' he said miserably. 'I couldn't bear to lose her. Just lately she's changed . . .' He broke off, fighting for breath.

Hastily I poured a brandy and put it into his hand. He was trembling violently. He muttered his thanks and, with an effort, raised the glass to his mouth.

I was wondering whether to phone for a doctor when the door bell gave two sharp rings. I had an instant of panic! If this should be Ericson the situation promised to be even more fantastic than my wild imaginings had supposed. It seemed certain that there would be at least one corpse for Mrs. Glover's satisfaction; Fairlee was already near to collapse and it seemed unlikely that he would survive the shock of coming face to face with Ericson at this moment.

As I flung open the front door a telegraph boy just managed to save himself from falling on to the mat. 'Sorry!' he said, with a sheepish grin. 'I was just having a look through the letter-box. I thought you weren't in.'

I took the telegram and ripped it open. I said there was no reply, gave the boy a shilling, and hastened back to the living room.

Fairlee was standing where I had left him, looking very woebegone and staring blankly at his empty glass.

'Are you feeling any better?' I asked, with genuine sympathy.

'I'm all right now, thanks to the brandy.' He smiled at me bleakly. 'I really shouldn't let myself get so excited.'

'No ... well – try not to worry too much, Fairlee,' I said reassuringly, taking the glass from his hand. 'I'm certain everything will be all right. Now, if you're sure you're well enough to get back home, will you excuse me? I've just had a wire calling me away.'

'Don't worry about me. These attacks look worse than they really are.' He squared his shoulders and swung his umbrella nonchalantly. 'Not bad news, I hope?'

'No. Just a rearranged meeting.'

At the front door he apologised again, then walked briskly off down the mews. I had the feeling that he was trying to impress me with his virility.

Back in the living room I re-read the telegram. It said:

WILL MEET YOU ELEVEN TONIGHT PARK CAR NEAR
QUEENSMERE POND WIMBLEDON WILL LOOK OUT FOR
YOU

DEMPSEY

I stuffed the telegram into my pocket, picked up my untouched drink and looked at it for a long moment. Then I took it out to the kitchen and poured it down the sink.

I was going to need a very clear head for the meeting at eleven.

5

It was ten past eleven when I arrived at the rendezvous. I was deliberately late because I wanted Dempsey to be first on the scene. If he were alone I'd decided that I would drive straight past him. He might well be the decoy to get me out of my car, leaving me wide open to attack; and I thought it unlikely that Ericson, as head of an international organisation, would move around without a substantial bodyguard. I had my gun with me, of course, but had no intention of using it except as a last resort. Attracting half a dozen police cars was definitely not on my agenda.

As it turned out, all my plans were wasted. No reception committee waited to greet me; the decoy was nowhere to be seen. Parking my car as close as possible to Queensmere Pond, I switched off the lights, made sure the car doors were locked, and waited for events to catch up with me.

It was a moonless night, with a trace of mist. Ideal, in fact, for any unpleasantness. I lit a cigarette and sat back, regretting that I hadn't filled a flask with whisky. Not that I was bored; I was constantly on the alert, and each time the headlamps of a car loomed up I kept carefully out of sight. I remembered the technique they'd used on Van Dakar and was taking no chances.

While I was waiting I contemplated my talk with Fairlee. Even making allowances for his jealous imaginings, it seemed fairly likely that the name Vivien Gilmore had mentioned on the telephone was Ericson's. What was less certain was that she'd been talking to Barbara.

I stubbed out my third cigarette. It seemed I'd been too clever in my calculations. It looked as though Dempsey and his associates had decided I didn't intend to keep the appointment and had taken themselves off before I arrived. Vaguely disappointed at having been denied any excitement I switched on the headlights and started the car.

I hadn't driven more than a few hundred yards before I saw the light of a torch being waved in the lane ahead. I slowed down, anticipating a trick. Then my headlamps caught the figure of a man leaning on a bicycle in the centre of the path. He was wearing the squat bowler hat, green jacket, and breeches of a Wimbledon Common Warden. I pulled up beside him, lowering the car window just sufficiently to ask what the trouble was.

'It's a man lying back there in the bushes,' the Warden told me. 'He's in a bad way – otherwise I wouldn't have stopped you.'

'What is it – a hit and run case?' I said. 'He looked more like he's been beaten up, sir,' the Warden said grimly. 'He needs hospital attention right away.'

I considered this for a moment, then said: 'I'll pull in to the side of the road, Warden. Then we'll go and look at this fellow. If he's not too badly hurt perhaps I could drive him down to Putney Hospital.'

When I'd moved my car I followed the Warden into the bushes, where a heavy figure lay on the turf, groaning, his head partly concealed by his arm. I stooped over him.

The sandy hair that usually spanned the bald dome was hanging over his left ear. The full-moon face, with the broad nose swollen and discoloured, and the wary eyes no longer capable of using a jeweller's eye-glass, stared up at me.

'Frazer . . . Is that you, Frazer?' His voice was little more than a whisper.

'Now don't worry, Dempsey – everything's going to be all right.' I tried to sound reassuring. 'We'll get you over to my car . . .'

'You know him, sir?' the Warden asked incredulously. 'Funny, isn't it – you just happening to come along like that and . . .'

'A lucky coincidence,' I said brusquely. 'Give me a hand to lift him over to my car, will you?'

Dempsey was a dead weight; it was like lifting a sack of flour. But we eventually had him propped up in the back seat of my car.

'Now, sir,' the Warden began in an official tone, dragging a notebook from his tunic pocket. 'It's my duty to report this to the police, so I'll have both your names and addresses, if you don't mind.'

I didn't need the groan of protest from the rear seat to tell me that I should make a quick get-away. 'My friend's an ulcer case. It may be critical. I must get him to the hospital right away,' I called urgently, engaging the gears. 'The hospital will give you our names. Give them a ring later. Good night, Warden. Thanks for all your help.'

'Good man, Frazer,' Dempsey muttered as we gathered speed.

'Good for *you*, you mean,' I called back. 'He'll have the number of my car! And save whatever breath you have left till we get back to my place.'

6

Somewhere on the drive back Dempsey lost consciousness. When I parked outside my flat he was breathing stertorously, his head lolling on the back of the seat. I dashed up to my flat, poured a half tumbler of brandy, and returned to the car.

Dempsey was stirring slightly. He opened the one eye which was still functioning. 'Milk . . . Frazer . . . milk . . .' he murmured.

I managed to get him over my shoulder and carry him into my flat. There I took off his jacket, loosened his tie, and lowered him into an armchair.

When I went out to the kitchen to get him a glass of milk and a sandwich I carried his jacket over my arm, and it wasn't until I'd looked through the pockets and found what I was looking for that I took it back to the living room, hung it over the back of a chair, and mixed myself a whisky and soda.

'How are you feeling?' I inquired, coming over and gazing down at him.

'I'm perking up,' he said. 'Thank God they didn't kick me in the stomach . . .'

His face was in a mess and there was a gash in his left temple which I judged had been caused by a lethally-aimed kick.

'Who are "they", Dempsey?'

'Gang of teenagers,' he said unconvincingly. There was an awkward pause as he took another bite at the sandwich. 'This is what the doctor ordered!' he chuckled, shedding crumbs onto the front of his crumpled shirt.

'So a gang of teenagers beat you up just for the fun of it?'

'They do that, you know.' He nodded sagely. 'But this lot were after my money. Turned out all my pockets.'

I crossed over to his jacket and took out his wallet. 'Well, they evidently missed that; and the fifty pounds inside.'

'Well, that's a stroke of luck!' he exclaimed. 'Maybe that Warden disturbed them. I wish he'd come sooner. Tomorrow I'll be so stiff I shan't be able to move.'

From his jacket pocket I took out two other articles and held them up. 'Then it looks as though you'll have to cancel this plane ticket to Montreal. I see you're due for a flight timed ten-thirty a.m.' I tossed the ticket on to his lap.

'What the hell are you up to, going through my pockets?' he snapped, his one serviceable eye watching me apprehensively. 'And what are you doing with my passport?'

'I'm keeping it, Dempsey. Whether you get it back depends on how co-operative you are.'

His reaction was surly. 'I'm not going to answer any questions,' he muttered. 'You're wasting your time, Frazer.'

I threw the passport on to a table. 'There's one thing more in the pocket of your jacket, Dempsey. A gun. That might interest the ballistic experts at the Yard. They've extracted the bullet from the man who was shot yesterday in a call-box in Lennard Street.'

'That wasn't me.' He levered himself up in the armchair, then fell back with a groan. 'I swear to God it wasn't.'

'You'll have to do better than that, Dempsey – otherwise I'm handing it over to the police. It is registered with them, I suppose?'

He gave a helpless sigh. 'All right,' he said tonelessly. 'What is it you want to know?'

'First, why did you come to meet me with a gun in your pocket? . . . Or shall I answer that?' I crossed to him, put a hand under his chin, and held up his face to mine. 'You were going to use it to force me to hand over the diamonds, weren't you? Your plan was to double-cross Ericson and get out of the country – wasn't it, Dempsey?'

'I paid for it, Frazer,' he moaned. 'They rumbled what I was up to and beat hell out of me.'

'Don't expect sympathy from me,' I said harshly. 'Was Ericson with them?'

'Ericson's too smart for that,' he said bitterly.

'But you know who Ericson is!' I persisted.

He shook his head, and a spasm of pain crossed his face. 'Those bastards never tell you anything.'

'Answer my question, Dempsey!' I said sharply. '*Who is Ericson?*'

'I don't know. I've never even spoken to him on the telephone. And that's the gospel truth!' He eyed me warily. 'Are you a detective, Frazer?'

'You know who I am, Dempsey; you were tipped off about me by telephone the first time I came to your office. We'll take it from there.' I looked down at him, thoughtfully. 'Your job in the set-up is to act as a go-between. The diamonds are stolen on the Continent and smuggled over by people like Cordwell. To prevent any slip-up the smuggler has to identify himself before being passed on to you. Am I right?'

'You said Cordwell told you all that. Why do we need to go over it all again?'

'I'm just verifying the facts,' I said equably. 'Now – if I were working for Ericson I should be supplied with a bulb catalogue, which I'd take to *The Dyke*, and they'd pass me on to you?'

'Jan made a false move there,' he said angrily. 'You'd never have got on to all this if the bloody fool hadn't given you that catalogue.'

'No doubt Ericson will take care of him.' I nodded. 'Now you tell me the rest.'

'I daren't, Frazer,' he replied with a shudder. 'You see what they've done to me already. Next time it'll be . . .' He drew a hand across his throat.

'All the more reason why you should tell me,' I said, picking up his passport from the table. 'You're going to need this very badly – but you're not getting it until you've come through with all the information I want.'

'For God's sake, Frazer! You've got to let me have that passport!' He shifted uneasily in the chair.

'Go on, Dempsey . . .'

I waited and at last he responded: 'When they're passed on to me I reel off a list of names. Among them is the code word. If they pick that out and repeat it, together with the code number . . .'

'Fantasy. Two-thirty,' I said, with a smile.

'How the hell you knew it beats me; it's changed every week.' He gave me a sly look. 'Where you came unstuck was on the last test.'

'Ah . . . the metronome.'

'That's right.' He extended a finger and waved it to and fro. 'You should have moved the pendulum to a certain number on the metronome scale. When you didn't do that, I knew you were a phoney.'

'Suppose I'd known the number – what then?'

'You'd have been passed on to somebody else.'

'Ericson?'

'Nobody gets passed on to Ericson.' He wiped his mouth with the back of his hand. 'Give me a break, Frazer. You wouldn't want them to kill me, would you?'

'You'd have killed me out there on Wimbledon Common,' I said savagely. 'Is Vivien Gilmore the go-between?'

He licked his lips nervously, then nodded.

'And it was she who warned you about me on the telephone?'

He nodded again.

'You say no one gets passed on to Ericson. Does Vivien Gilmore settle the deal?'

'Yes.' He plucked at the arm of the chair.

I half filled a tumbler with brandy and handed it to him. It was not entirely a gesture of solicitude, for I was relying on the brandy to loosen his tongue.

He gulped down most of it, then looked up at me contritely.

'You've got me wrong, Frazer. I wouldn't have used the gun on you tonight. It was only meant as a threat.'

'I'll take your word for it,' I said, dropping into a chair opposite his.

Presently, he said: 'You know something, Frazer? After the way they beat me up, I'd shop them all.'

I decided this was to be the moment of truth, and that now was the time for me to ask: 'What do you know about a man called Leo Salinger?'

'I've heard of him,' he admitted. 'He was killed in a car accident in Amsterdam.'

'And the stolen diamonds that were . . .'

'Leo knew nothing about the diamonds,' he interposed. 'They were hidden in a metronome that Salinger was carrying, but as far as he was concerned he was just delivering a birthday present to a friend of his brother's.'

'His brother?'

'That's right – Arnold Salinger. Arnold often brought diamonds over to Ericson, but at that particular time he was laid up with a broken ankle, so Arnold hit on the idea of hiding the diamonds in the metronome and asking Leo to deliver them.'

'But Leo never got here.'

'He was knocked down when he was on his way to the airport. The metronome vanished. I heard that Ericson was furious about the whole business. He thought Arnold was double-crossing him. He put the pressure on the poor devil, and Arnold finished up by committing suicide.'

'How do you think Cordwell got hold of the missing diamonds?'

Dempsey shrugged. 'He must have known Leo Salinger was carrying them. Maybe Arnold told him. Cordwell probably decided to follow Leo and wait for his chance to knock off the metronome. Anyhow, he came over here and tried to do a deal with Ericson . . . You know what happened.'

This sounded remarkably like the answer to Ross's problem. But I still persisted.

'Barbara Day was driving the car that killed Leo Salinger. Now, tell me what you know about her.'

'I told you before, Frazer – the name means nothing to me. But knowing names isn't encouraged in Ericson's outfit. I know Vivien Gilmore's because I have to contact her when someone comes into my office with a packet of stolen diamonds. As a cover she runs an antique shop.'

'With Barbara Day,' I said, more to myself than to Dempsey.

'Cordwell was murdered in Barbara Day's flat, wasn't he?' Dempsey scratched his head. 'Ericson suspected Cordwell of selling diamonds to some other set-up. If you ask me, that's why Cordwell was murdered.'

'By Ericson, personally?'

'Possibly.'

'Did you pass on the word that I wanted to do a deal with him?'

'Yes, through Vivien Gilmore. I don't know what made him suspect I was up to something. I told Vivien you'd be bringing the diamonds.'

'Strange that Ericson didn't set his gang of thugs on to me, then.'

'That's what I thought. You had a lucky break there, Frazer. But they'll catch up with you before long. You watch your step, Mister – you wouldn't want to finish up like Cordwell, would you?'

'You can say that again!'

'Well,' he said after a pause, 'do I get my passport?'

The telephone rang. I picked up the receiver, watching Dempsey as a female voice drawled in my ear. 'Oh, Mr. Frazer – this is Vivien Gilmore. I'd very much like to see you . . . Could you be at *The Dyke* at ten o'clock tomorrow morning?'

'I think I can manage that, Miss Gilmore.'

She cut in on me hastily: 'Don't mention this to anyone, Mr. Frazer – particularly Barbara. Ten tomorrow, then. That's a date.'

As I replaced the receiver Dempsey said: 'What did she want?'

'She wants to see me.'

'What did I tell you!' he said knowingly. 'Your number's in the frame, Frazer! I've warned you . . . Well – what about my passport?'

'It's all yours,' I said, pushing it across the table towards him.

He picked it up and slipped it into his hip pocket. 'And would you do me a favour?' he asked. 'Phone for a taxi. I'll never make it to the underground.'

I dialled the rank in Knightsbridge.

'That's okay, Dempsey,' I said presently, 'It'll be here in

five minutes. I should have a hot bath and a couple of aspirin tonight. And be sure you catch that plane tomorrow morning.'

'You can bet on it!' He lifted his jacket from the chair, groaning as he tried to put it on. 'Could you give me a hand?'

As I helped him, I took the gun from the jacket pocket. It was a .38 automatic. 'I wouldn't be caught landing in Montreal with this, if I were you, Dempsey. I'm told the Canadian police can be pretty rough with gunmen.'

'You're welcome to it. And good luck to you, Frazer. No hard feelings, I hope.'

'You're an optimist,' I said, steering him to the door. 'There's your taxi now.'

7

As I was leaving my flat the next morning I walked straight into Inspector Trueman.

'I'd just like a word with you, sir,' he said, edging me back into the flat. 'I shan't keep you a moment.'

'You'd better not,' I said. 'I've an appointment in twenty minutes' time.'

In the living room Mrs. Glover was gathering up my breakfast tray. 'Would the gentleman like a cup of coffee, Mr. Frazer?' she inquired.

I told her the visitor wasn't staying and she took the hint.

'You wouldn't be able to get rid of a wife as easily as that,'

Trueman said enviously when Mrs. Glover had gone. 'There are times when I wish I was a bachelor again, sir.'

'Why? A policeman can always find an excuse for being out late. I should think you have the best of both worlds, Inspector.'

'Odd you should mention being out late,' he said, lifting an eyebrow. 'What time did you get back last night, sir?'

'So that Warden did get the number of my car,' I said urbanely. 'Well, what is it you want to know?'

'The name of the man you *said* you were going to drive to the hospital.'

'He was a friend of mine. I brought him back here. All he needed was a brandy.'

'According to our information he was badly beaten up. Do you know why he was beaten up, sir?'

'If I knew that, Inspector, the problem of juvenile delinquents would be solved.'

'Teddy boys, eh? That's what the Warden thought.' He eyed me quizzically. 'Quite a coincidence his being a friend of yours, wasn't it?'

'I'm plagued with coincidences. A man is murdered, and my fingerprints turn up on the door.' I laughed. 'That's the sort of coincidence I'm always running up against.'

'I shouldn't let it happen too often, sir. It could prove awkward.'

'Such as my being suspected of murder, for instance?'

'You're not under any suspicion in the Cordwell murder, Mr. Frazer,' he informed me somewhat reluctantly. 'Although we do think you know who did it.' He studied his hat-band carefully. 'It's a serious offence to withhold evidence that could assist the police in their inquiries.'

'What makes you think I would defy the police?'

'You seem to be very friendly with the lady who occupies the flat where the body was found, Mr. Frazer. Women do tend to confide in . . . well, a rather special man, you know, sir.'

'I do know some of the facts of life, Inspector. But if there's any "special" man, as you so discreetly call it, in Miss Day's life, it's the man she's engaged to.'

'I saw Mr. Fairlee just before coming here. He tells me the engagement is broken off. I gathered he wasn't too happy about your friendship with Miss Day.'

'That's strange . . . When he was here yesterday he gave me the impression that he thought *you* were being rather over-zealous in your visits to her . . . But I shouldn't let it worry you, Inspector.'

'I shan't,' he assured me. 'Though you'd be surprised how careful a policeman has to be sometimes. A woman as attractive as Miss Day, for instance, can lead you right up the garden path.'

'Well, I'm not a policeman . . .'

'You do mix with some rather strange people,' he countered, and I presumed he was referring to Richards.

'I have many friends,' I said. 'I don't always ask them how they earn their living.'

'As a policeman, it's the first thing I want to know. We're always interested in a man who has no known occupation.' He rubbed his chin. 'You fall into that category, sir.'

'For your police records I'm an engineer by profession, temporarily engaged in journalistic work. Does that satisfy you?'

'It doesn't explain why you have so much free time, Mr. Frazer. Or what you do with it.'

'What's all this leading up to?'

'Just this, sir. I suggest you leave police business to those who are paid to do it.'

'Why should you think I dabble in police business?' I challenged.

'You're too interested in the Cordwell murder, sir. And if you'll take my advice, you'll keep clear of it. Cordwell was mixed up with some unpleasant characters who can be very nasty indeed with anyone who crosses their path. I'm warning you, Mr. Frazer.'

'Thanks, Inspector. By the way, did you ever trace this Ericson you've been questioning us about?'

'We know that Ericson is the head of the stolen diamond organisation that Cordwell was working for. That's as far as we've got.' He gave me a penetrating stare. 'Why did you ask that?'

'I was curious, that's all.'

'Then I advise you to restrain your curiosity, sir.' He walked to the door, then turned. 'And if you do happen to get to know anything more about Ericson, telephone *me* – at once! That's an order, Mr. Frazer! Otherwise you may find yourself charged with obstructing the police. I don't care who's behind you,' he went on emphatically, 'I'll make it my business to see that you get six months! I mean that.'

From the look on his face I was sure that he did.

As I took a taxi to Lennard Street I wondered just how much pull Ross had with the police – and whether or not he'd use it on my behalf if it came to a showdown. I had an unpleasant feeling that he wouldn't.

8

Vivien was talking to Jan when I arrived at *The Dyke*, and as she caught sight of me the smile faded from her face. He followed her eyes and, turning quickly, hurried behind the counter.

I crossed to her table and sat down. As I did so Jan left the counter and quickly locked the door, deftly switching the 'Open' sign to 'Closed'.

As I watched him I heard Vivien saying: 'Would you like a coffee, Mr. Frazer?

'No, thank you,' I replied, still keeping a wary eye on Jan. Without a glance at us he returned to the counter. 'Well, what is it you want to see me about?' I asked Vivien.

She dropped a lump of sugar into her coffee, and stirred it slowly. 'I'm worried about Barbara,' she replied, with a rueful smile. 'She's broken off her engagement.'

'Why should that worry you?' I asked, making no effort to keep the sarcasm out of my voice.

'Arthur's making such a nuisance of himself, running her nerves ragged, trying to get her to change her mind.'

'How did you expect him to take it?'

'I thought you might talk to Barbara,' she said. 'She listens to you. If you can just convince her she's done the right thing . . .'

I regarded her with some amusement. 'Is that why you asked me here this morning, simply to persuade me to bolster your friend's morale?'

Her eyes hardened. 'It wasn't the main reason.'

'Then why don't we come to the main reason?'

She glanced across at Jan, then lowered her voice. 'I want the diamonds,' she said coolly.

I effected a look of surprise. 'What diamonds?'

'Let's not play games,' she replied, her tone hardening. 'I know you have the Cordwell diamonds.'

I laughed incredulously. 'What the hell's got into you, Vivien? Do you mean to say Cordwell really was carrying diamonds?'

'You know he was.' She looked over to Jan and nodded. 'All right, Jan.'

He reached under the counter and produced a tape recorder, then pressed the starting switch. I recognised Dempsey's voice immediately.

'How much do you want for them, Frazer?'

'Not a middle-man's price. But I'll do a deal with your boss.'

'Who said I had a boss?'

'Cordwell.'

I listened to a little more of that familiar conversation, then Vivien nodded at Jan once more and he obediently switched off the tape recorder. There was a pause.

'So you didn't trust Dempsey,' I said at last.

'Ericson didn't. But then Ericson doesn't trust anyone. Not even me.'

'Apparently he trusts you to buy diamonds for him,' I said. 'Well, Vivien, how much are you prepared to pay?'

'I'm not prepared to pay anything,' she said coldly. 'Just hand them over to me, and we'll consider the matter closed.'

'And supposing I don't hand them over, Vivien?'

She shrugged. 'We'll simply tell the police you have them. That, coupled with the fact that your fingerprints were found in Barbara's flat, will put you really on the spot.'

'As Cordwell's murderer, you mean?' I said. 'Is that what you're trying to pin on me? Play through the rest of that tape. Then you'll hear how I happened to be in the flat.'

'I have played it through, Tim. Do you think the police will swallow that story of the key being slipped under the door?'

'How would I have got in otherwise?'

'The same way Cordwell got in – up the fire-escape.'

'And why would he go up that way?' I said incredulously. 'Somebody inside the flat let him in.'

So Barbara hasn't told you what really did happen?' She gave a short laugh. 'Then I'll tell you. You see, Cordwell had a sideline to his diamond smuggling.'

'Blackmail?'

She nodded. 'He picked up your camera at *De Kroon*, probably accidentally. Then when he'd run the film through, he thought he had a film he could use to blackmail Barbara. He'd discovered she had a jealous fiancé who'd be livid when he knew another man had taken such an interest in her.'

'There's a perfectly innocent explanation. Hasn't Barbara told you?'

'About you wanting an attractive girl in your pictures of Amsterdam?' She laughed again. 'Barbara's a damn little idiot to fall for that! But to get back to Cordwell – he phoned Barbara to find out how much she'd pay for the film. She thought he was crazy and refused to buy the film from him. So he entered her flat by way of the fire-escape to try and scare her into doing a deal.'

'How do you know all this?' I countered. 'Were you there at the time?'

'It's obvious. Barbara went to Arthur's – you followed Cordwell and went up the fire-escape after him. You knew he had the diamonds on him. You told Dempsey as much, and it's on the tape recorder, don't forget. You can't wriggle out this time.'

Richards was right. It had been a mistake to tell Dempsey I was in the flat that night. 'I was there,' I admitted, 'but Cordwell was already dead. He was murdered by whoever slipped the key to me.'

'Who'll believe that? Not the police, you can be sure. You give me the diamonds and I'll have that tape recording erased.'

'You work for Ericson,' I said. 'I dragged that out of Dempsey yesterday evening, after he'd been beaten up.' I glanced at my watch. Dempsey would be on his way to Montreal by now. 'Yes,' I said guiltily, 'I was in the flat, and I answered the phone when you rang to warn Barbara that someone was curious about Ericson and Lennard Street.'

She nodded. 'But the "someone" was Fairlee. Don't try to pin anything on Barbara, Tim. She's just a damn little fool who can't make up her mind.'

'Then why that call about Ericson? If she's not mixed up with him, why the warning?'

'Ericson has seen me with Barbara. He's fallen for her, and he wanted me to arrange for him to meet her here at *The Dyke*. Fairlee came into the shop one day while Barbara was out, and said he'd overheard her making arrangements to meet someone. That's why I phoned Barbara on the night of the murder – to warn her that Fairlee was getting suspicious.'

'Tell me – did Barbara ever meet Ericson?' I asked.

'Never,' she said emphatically. 'Nor does she know anything about the diamond set-up.'

Though I was far from satisfied I didn't want any further argument. 'All right, Vivien,' I said, 'I'll accept your explanation. But you can tell Ericson that I want twelve thousand pounds for those diamonds. They're worth a great deal more, and I've no doubt he'll make a nice profit. I want twelve thousand, not a penny less and I want it from Ericson himself.'

She stared at me suspiciously. 'You wouldn't be working for the police, would you, Tim?'

'Does it sound like it,' I retorted quickly, 'when I'm offering stolen diamonds for sale? But if Ericson doesn't come through with twelve thousand I'll tip the police off about you. So you'd better do some fast talking.'

She considered this for a few minutes, then said: 'I'll try to arrange for Ericson to meet you, I promise you that.' Then her mouth tightened. 'But I promise you something else. You'll get a beating up later that will make you think Dempsey's was fun and games with the kindergarten class.'

I made it obvious that this threat didn't bother me at all.

As I moved to the door I took Jan aside.

'You'd better think up an alibi for eleven o'clock last night.' I advised. 'The police are looking for the thugs who beat up a man on Wimbledon Common at about that time. Before I go to meet Ericson I shall write a letter to Inspector Trueman telling him to call in here if I should be away from my flat for longer than twenty-four hours. You might keep that in mind, Jan.'

'He can have a coffee on the house,' Jan said threateningly. 'While he's listening to that tape recording, Mr. Frazer.'

'Then maybe he'll let you hear a recording of my conversation with Dempsey after he was beaten up last night,' I said, grinning at him. 'Your name crops up in it several times . . . I'll leave the "Closed" notice on the door,' I said casually as I put my hand on the latch. 'I've an idea it'll be there for a long, long time. Good morning, Jan.'

I went out, reflecting with some amusement that, for a Dutchman, Jan's command of obscene English was remarkable.

CHAPTER TWENTY

I

Richards was pacing up and down the mews when I got back. As I got out of the taxi I asked the driver to wait ten minutes, then drive me to Chelsea.

'Bet you a drink I know the address,' Richards said, at my elbow. 'It'll be 23 Crawford House Mansions, driver.'

'That wasn't funny, Richards,' I said irritably, as we went into my flat.

'Frazer, the job you were assigned to do is completed,' Richards said firmly. 'Why chase around after Barbara Day, trying to solve a murder that's no concern of yours?'

'She's invited me round to her flat for lunch. Do I have to ask Ross's permission?'

'He's in the mood to say "yes" to anything you ask him. As a matter of fact, that's why I've called. He wants me to pass on his congratulations for the way you've handled the Salinger case. But now that we know Salinger was innocent of any connection with Ericson, the case is closed.'

'Not so far as I'm concerned,' I said. 'In the engineering trade we learn to see the job through. And I shan't have finished this one until I've found out who Ericson is.'

'Very noble sentiments, Frazer. But I'm afraid they don't impress me.'

'Exactly what do you mean by that, Richards?' I said angrily.

He shook his head reproachfully. 'Am I right in thinking you're trying to prove that Barbara Day had nothing to do with the murder of Cordwell?'

'What if I am?' I said, throwing my hat into a chair. 'Is there anything against helping a girl out of a damned awkward situation?'

'And if you establish she's the sweet, innocent thing that you imagine, what then? What sort of reward are you expecting, eh?'

'Your trouble is, you're a romantic, Richards,' I said testily.

'My trouble is, I'm just a cynic who likes to collect his bets when he wins.'

'All right, Richards,' I said. 'Help yourself to a drink.'

He did so, then looked up at me and said seriously: 'You're on dangerous ground, you know, Frazer.'

'I know,' I said. 'And I'm seeing this thing through, Richards. I'm making an appointment to see Ericson, and I'm hoping to sell him those diamonds for twelve thousand pounds.'

He gave a long, soft whistle. 'I suppose you know – quite apart from the fact that the diamonds don't belong to you – that dealing in stolen property is a criminal offence? Are you asking me to compound a felony by giving you the go-ahead?'

'I'm playing the cards my own way,' I said airily. 'All I want to do is to meet Ericson; the diamonds are only a bait. My aim is to find Cordwell's murderer.' I went on, not very convincingly: 'And everything points to it being Ericson. When that elusive individual is behind bars I'll call it a day on the Salinger case.'

'Better retire from this case on your laurels,' advised Richards. 'You're Ross's blue-eyed boy at the moment.'

'Unfinished business never did satisfy me,' I said obstinately. 'Anyway, I'm curious to know who Ericson is.'

'You can let me know when and where you're meeting him, Frazer,' Richards said dryly. 'Van Dakar wasn't so well when I phoned the hospital this morning. He's pretty weak.'

'That's another reason for bringing Ericson to justice,' I said vehemently. 'All right. I promise to let you know where and when the meeting is to be. Does that satisfy you?'

'It may save me having to dig into my pocket for a subscription to a wreath!'

My taxi driver was stamping up and down the mews when I came out of the building a few minutes later.

'Jump in, guv!' he said, and we drove off swiftly, leaving Richards staring after me with a resigned expression.

At Crawford House Mansions I paid off the taxi and went up in the lift to the second floor.

When I rang the bell, Barbara opened the door and seemed relieved to see me. 'Vivien's here,' she said, 'and Arthur's just phoned. He's become an absolute pest.'

'About your breaking off the engagement?' I queried sympathetically.

'So he's been to see you?' Barbara said, leading the way into the living room.

'He's been to see me all right!' I ejaculated. 'He practically accused me of being the man responsible.'

I nodded to Vivien, who was sprawled in an easy chair. She gave me a meaning look.

The telephone rang, and Barbara made a gesture of impatience. 'That's probably him. I'll take it in my bedroom, if you don't mind, Tim.'

I nodded understandingly, and she went into the bedroom.

Vivien looked after her, then turned to me. 'I've arranged the meeting with Ericson for tonight. In Maida Vale.'

'So he's prepared to do a deal?'

'He's agreed to your price. He'll meet you at Number 3 Monkton Villas.'

I pulled out my diary. 'Just a minute, I'll make a note of that,' I said, remembering Richards' advice about jotting down addresses.

'And come alone,' Vivien added quickly. 'If there's anyone with you the deal is off.'

'I'll come alone,' I reassured her.

'Ericson will be watching to make sure of that. You can't miss the house. It has a "To Let" board outside.' She took a Yale key from her handbag and handed it to me. 'Just let yourself in. It's empty, so you won't be disturbed . . .'

I regarded her thoughtfully. 'What assurance have I that Ericson will hand over the money, or that I'll come out of that house alive, for that matter?' I asked.

'You haven't any assurance,' she said smoothly. 'But presumably you thought of that contingency when you asked for this meeting.'

I smiled and nodded. 'When I get back to my flat I'm going to write a letter. I shall address it to Inspector Trueman, and hand it over to my Bank Manager with very definite instructions. I'm sure I don't have to tell you what those instructions will be, Vivien. If anything happens to me tonight, that letter will be delivered to Scotland Yard tomorrow morning. You might pass on that information to Ericson.'

'I will.' She laughed. 'But I think you're in for a surprise, Tim.'

'Maybe Ericson is due for a surprise himself,' I suggested, pocketing the key. 'What time do I see him?'

'At midnight.' She glanced at her wristwatch. 'And that reminds me, I have an appointment in ten minutes. Do apologise to Barbara for me.'

A few minutes later Barbara came into the room. She nodded without speaking when I told her that Vivien had left; she seemed depressed, and sank into an easy chair.

'Arthur is driving me frantic,' she said presently. 'He's threatening to commit suicide, among other things.'

'Oh, he'll get over it. But you must be quite firm and refuse to see him.' I leaned back in my chair. 'Incidentally, after first accusing *me* of having an affair with you, he switched the blame on to the man called Ericson. I tried to tell him you didn't know anyone of that name. You don't – do you, Barbara?'

'No, I don't,' she said, hesitating, her eyes on my face. 'I don't know him, but . . . well, you see, Ericson is a friend of Vivien's, and I thought if I told Trueman that . . . well . . .' She broke off with a little shrug.

'Go on . . .'

'I thought the police would be sure to think she had some connection with Cordwell.'

'And had she any connection with Cordwell?' I persisted.

'No. No, I'm sure she hadn't,' Barbara said with conviction.

'Have you known Vivien long?' I asked her.

'Quite a while.' She locked her hands behind her head and half closed her eyes. 'Arthur introduced us, as a matter of fact.'

'Did you know anything about her before you met?'

'Not much,' she said with some reluctance. 'She knew a lot of people with money who were interested in antiques. So, naturally, I thought she would be quite an asset as a partner in my business.' She caught my eye and said: 'She might be useful to you if you're needing some capital to start up your business again. Why don't you have a talk with her?'

'I'd need twelve thousand,' I said dubiously. 'That's quite a lot of money, if you haven't any security to offer.'

'I suppose it is,' she said. 'Haven't you any security?'

I shook my head and gently brought the conversation back to Ericson. 'Did Cordwell ever mention Ericson to you?' I inquired. Then I added, suddenly: 'You know that Cordwell was dealing in stolen diamonds, don't you, Barbara?'

She looked startled. 'No . . . No, I didn't know,' she said quietly. 'Trueman said he was a blackmailer, but I didn't think . . .'

I wanted to believe her. Vivien Gilmore must have been lying when she'd told me Barbara knew about Cordwell's other activities; she'd obviously used it as an excuse to introduce the subject of the diamonds.

'You're not trying to warn me against Vivien, are you, Tim?' she said anxiously. 'I've always trusted her – I'd hate to think she was mixed up in anything like that.'

'No, I didn't mean that,' I said hastily. 'But Vivien knowing Ericson, and Trueman being so obviously suspicious of him – well, it made me curious about her background.'

'Really, you're as bad as Arthur!' she protested. 'He's always warning me not to trust her.'

'There's another possibility, Barbara. Do you think Cordwell came here that night to try to blackmail you?'

'Blackmail me! But how could he? There was nothing he could blackmail me about.'

'There was the film they found in his pocket – the film I took of you in Amsterdam. Fairlee might have been jealous if he'd known I was following you around.'

'I must say it did look as though you had more than a casual interest in me, Tim,' she admitted, smiling. She sat up in her chair. 'But how did Cordwell get hold of that film? I remember you telling the Inspector you lost it somewhere. Cordwell must have stolen it.' She stood up, with a despairing gesture. 'Oh, I can't bear any more of this. Ever since that car accident I've had a feeling I was being followed. There was a man in Amsterdam who followed me everywhere. Wherever I went I'd see him – in museums, art galleries . . . Then you – when you were taking pictures of me – and then Cordwell being murdered in my flat – and this constant questioning by that detective . . .'

Impulsively, I put my hand on her shoulder. 'Tell me the

truth, Barbara; have you ever met Ericson?' I asked gently. She raised her head and met my eyes without flinching.

'Ericson means nothing to me – nothing at all, Tim. Can't you understand that?'

Reassured, I smiled down at her. 'I'm meeting Ericson tonight. Vivien has arranged it.'

She shook her head. 'You mustn't keep that appointment. I'm sure something dreadful will happen.'

'What makes you say that?' I asked sharply.

'I just feel it,' she said miserably. 'Vivien has some object in all this. I don't know what it is. But it's dreadful to feel oneself surrounded by all this suspicion . . . Tim, I just have to get away for a bit. I have a cottage in Cornwall – at St. Mawes, overlooking the harbour. It's so quiet there.' She smiled up at me. 'Can you sail a boat, Tim?'

I nodded. 'I used to,' I said. 'At Burnham-on-Crouch. I used to go there sometimes when I had a lot of business problems. Somehow, in a boat my worries didn't seem quite so important . . .'

She held out her hand, tentatively. 'Why don't you come with me, Tim? Then we could get all this unpleasant affair into its proper perspective. Will you, Tim?'

It sounded very tempting.

Her eyes softened. 'I'll have everything packed tomorrow morning. We could catch the ten-thirty from Paddington. Can you call for me here?'

I said I would, and she gave a little sigh of satisfaction. 'And, please, don't go to meet Ericson tonight . . . Promise me that . . .'

I shook my head. 'I want to clear up this Cordwell business, Barbara, for your sake. Until that's settled there can be no peace of mind for you. Don't worry, Barbara, when next we meet I hope to have everything cleared up.'

'Then take care of yourself,' she urged. 'Promise me, Tim?'

As I promised I touched the gun in my jacket pocket, just for luck.

2

The thought of the gun in my pocket comforted me once again as I walked along the deserted Maida Vale street, peering at the tall, late-Victorian houses of Monkton Villas. Most of them were shabby and in need of a coat of paint, and Number 3, with a 'To Let' board leaning out over a scrubby privet hedge, was no exception.

I walked up the steps to the paint-peeling door and inserted the key into the lock. The door creaked as I pushed it open, and I stepped into a stuffy-smelling hallway.

I switched on my small torch and looked round the meagrely furnished hall. There was a door on the right, opposite the foot of the stairs. I stood and listened for a moment or two; if Ericson had arrived there was no sign of his presence. Carefully, I turned the door-knob and slowly pushed open the door.

At first glance it looked like an ordinary living room: the furniture was covered with dust sheets, and I could detect the familiar shapes of chairs, a sideboard, and a writing bureau.

Swivelling the torch beam over a wide radius, I began to advance across the room. It seemed like any other room awaiting the removal men – until the beam of my torch suddenly lit up a man's foot.

The foot was turned upwards, and as the torchlight probed further into the darkness I discovered that the owner of the foot was lying behind the settee, apparently unconscious.

My first reaction was to switch off the torch and stand perfectly still, listening for the sound of his breathing. A shaft of light from a street lamp on the opposite side of the road shone weakly through the side of the old-fashioned bay window; the room was still eerily quiet, nor was there any sound from any other part of the house.

Making up my mind at last, I took a couple of quick steps, put one knee on the settee and, leaning over the back, shone the torch behind. What I saw made me go round the settee at once to take a closer look . . .

The pale face and sandy hair were only too familiar. Dempsey hadn't used his passport to get to Montreal, it seemed. He would never use it again.

There was a heavy crimson smear on his left temple and a trickle of blood from his mouth. Obviously there was nothing I could do for him this time . . . I straightened myself and as my head came above the level of the back of the settee the beam from a powerful torch caught me squarely in the eyes.

It was a few seconds before I could distinguish the figure in the doorway. Standing there, with the torch in his left hand and what looked like a .38 automatic in his right, was Arthur

Fairlee. He had removed his glasses, and his staring eyes were cold and menacing.

I waited for him to break the silence, but he did not speak. 'I came here to meet Ericson,' I said at last, through dry lips.

'That's a damned lie!' Fairlee said hotly. 'You'd arranged to meet Barbara here.'

I gripped the back of the settee.

'Switch off that torch and put your hands up!' he ordered, and it seemed safer to obey. His face was strangely contorted as he said: 'Why the hell couldn't you stick to the job you were hired for, and leave Barbara alone?'

'What was the job I was hired for?' I asked edging forward.

'To uncover the diamond racket, wasn't it?' he said, gripping the butt of the gun. 'Vivien's been on to you ever since you went to see Dempsey.'

'I've brought you the diamonds,' I said, lowering my arm and feeling for the jewel box in my waistcoat pocket. 'Have you brought the twelve thousand pounds?'

'Keep your distance!' he said sharply. 'No, I haven't brought the twelve thousand. Do you think that *I'm* Ericson?'

'No, I don't,' I said. 'Don't be a fool, Fairlee. The people I work for won't let you get away with murdering me. Put that gun away and you can have the diamonds.'

'You're in no position to bargain, Frazer,' he said, taking a pace towards me. 'You're going to die – not only because you know too much, but because you took Barbara from me.'

'Wait a minute, Fairlee,' I said, opening the jewel case. 'Trueman's getting damned close to finding Cordwell's murderer.

If you have any sense you'll leave the country as soon as you can. You'll need money. Here, take these diamonds and sell them to Ericson.' I held out the box, letting the light shine onto the stones. 'They can buy you your freedom. Otherwise, you'll get a fifteen years' sentence at least.'

The gun in his hand wavered. He leaned forward, his eyes focused on the box. I brought my hand up with all my weight behind it, the diamonds hitting him directly between the eyes.

As he staggered back I swung my other arm against his gun, knocking it from his hand. As I made a dive for it he came down on me with an upward knee-thrust. Then his fingers closed round my throat with the vicious clutch of a near-maniac. In a desperate attempt to escape those choking fingers I heaved my body upwards, throwing Fairlee over my head. His hands left my throat but he grabbed at the gun. Then he was kneeling over me, the gun pointed between my eyes. There was a sudden crack, and I thought for a moment that the explosion was the bullet crashing into my skull. Then I realised that the gun itself had dropped on my forehead, and the blood I could feel on my face was dripping from Fairlee's wrist. I rolled over, and saw the figure of a tall, lean man looking down at me.

'Doesn't do too badly for a sick man, does he?' said Richards' imperturbable voice.

'Thanks, Richards!' I managed to say breathlessly, as I struggled to my feet. I indicated the settee. 'I was luckier than Dempsey, poor devil!'

'Yes, we know about him,' Richards said quietly. 'They'd already dealt with Dempsey when I arrived on the scene.'

'Yes, just what *are* you doing here, Richards?' I asked, still trying to get my breath back.

'Our department isn't a suicide squad, Frazer,' he answered smoothly. 'When you were so adamant about meeting Ericson I simply decided to keep an eye on things.'

'M'm . . .' I said reflectively. 'So that's what was in your mind when you insisted on knowing the time and place.'

He smiled, and picked up Fairlee's gun, wrapping it in his handkerchief. 'This will interest Scotland Yard, I daresay,' he said to Fairlee, who was binding his own handkerchief round his injured wrist. 'Inspector Trueman should be here at any moment. I put a call through to the Yard directly I'd found Dempsey.'

'It's lucky for me you came back here when you did,' I said. 'Thanks again!'

'A pleasure,' he said, and added casually: 'Don't forget the diamonds, Frazer. Ross will dock their value out of my salary if I don't return them . . .'

I laughed, retrieved the diamonds, and handed the box to Richards. A police car drew up outside the house.

'Come on, Frazer.'

As we went down the pathway Inspector Trueman got out of the car. 'I'll want a word with you tomorrow, Mr. Frazer,' he said as he passed me.

'Make it ten o'clock,' I said. 'At 23 Crawford House Mansions. It may be rather urgent.'

'I'll have two of my men there,' Trueman said, turning. 'We don't want anyone going down the fire escape this time, do we, sir?'

3

At ten minutes to ten next morning I rang the bell outside Barbara's flat. She opened the door, wearing a fur coat over the shoulders of a dark suit.

'That's what you were wearing the first day I met you, Barbara,' I said. 'Remember, on the plane to Amsterdam?'

She nodded, her eyes shining. 'Did you imagine I'd forget?' She kissed me lightly on the cheek and gestured at the suitcase in the hall. 'I've been up since seven . . . packing.'

She waited for me to come in and close the door, then went on: 'Am I glad to see you! I tried to telephone you to make sure you'd be here, but you were out.'

'I told you I'd come,' I said quietly.

'Yes, I know.' She sighed. 'But I've been involved in so many panics lately. And, of course, Vivien is simply running round in circles. It'll be wonderful to get away from it all.' She smiled and held out her hand to me, then moved one of her cases out of the way. 'Tim, where's your luggage?' she queried suddenly.

'It's outside . . . in my car . . .' I stalled.

She glanced a her wristwatch. 'There's just time for a coffee, if you'd like one?'

I shook my head and she seemed to sense the tension in my manner.

'Is anything the matter?' she asked.

I indicated the door of the living room. 'Can we go inside for a few minutes?'

She stood with her back to the fireplace, facing me. I was momentarily at a loss, but finally managed to say: 'I'm not going away with you, Barbara.'

She caught her breath sharply and put out a hand to clutch the back of a chair. 'Then why did you come?' she demanded, as I moved a couple of paces towards her.

'To meet Ericson,' I replied quietly.

She stared at me for some seconds without speaking. There was no sound in the room except the muffled throb of a pneumatic drill some distance down the street.

'You expect to meet Ericson here?' she said in an incredulous tone.

I nodded. 'Arthur Fairlee's made a full statement to the police. They know about the diamonds and why Cordwell came here to see you. They know how Fairlee murdered him, then pushed the key under the door so that I could let myself in and leave my fingerprints.'

'It isn't true!' she protested, but I went on unheeding.

'You both left by the fire-escape, then you came back alone through the front door and put on a very convincing performance. Was that why you invited me – to provide an audience?'

'No, Tim,' she said simply. 'It was an accident – you've got to believe that.'

'Then why did you ask me round to your flat that night?'

'I asked you so that Arthur could take a look at you. I knew you'd been following me in Amsterdam. I thought perhaps if you were in the diamond business Arthur might recognise you.'

'So there was no intention of murdering Cordwell in the first place?'

'No. No, he just turned up out of the blue – and then when he started his blackmailing threats I'm afraid Arthur lost all control . . . However, it turned out rather well, except for the diamonds.' She fidgeted with the strip of braid on the back of the upholstered chair. 'What made you think of looking for them in the cigar-holder?'

'It's my job to think of things like that,' I replied evasively. The cards were on the table now, and I was watching her closely for the first sign of any suspicious move. 'I can't understand you, Barbara,' I said helplessly. 'You killed Leo Salinger because you thought his brother Arnold was double-crossing you and that Leo was making off with the diamonds; you were responsible for the suicide of Arnold Salinger; you involved your best friend in diamond smuggling, and your fiancé in murder . . . Why did you do it?'

She regarded me distantly for a long moment, then said quite calmly: 'Because I happen to be Ericson.'

4

For a brief moment I hesitated, then went out into the hall and opened the front door. Trueman was waiting outside, as I'd expected, and together we returned to the living room. As we entered, Barbara was picking up her handbag.

'I always knew there would be an end to all this,' she said, nodding towards the Inspector. 'But it will be my way, not theirs.'

As Trueman crossed to the bedroom and called to the policeman on the fire-escape she drew a small automatic from her handbag. 'Don't touch me!' she said, levelling the gun at Trueman. The policeman came in from the bedroom, a grizzled, elderly man, in a flat squad-car hat. He was plainly startled at the sight of the gun. 'Stand over by the Inspector,' Barbara ordered, waving it at him threateningly. 'I'll use this, you know.'

'Do as she says, Sergeant,' Trueman said suavely. 'There's no sense in starting anything.'

Barbara slid her hand into her bag again and took out a small red-capped phial. 'I'm going into my bedroom now,' she said quietly. 'Don't follow me, Tim – now or later. I don't want you to see me again.'

I heard a strained voice, which I had difficulty in recognising as my own, saying. 'Barbara, don't be a fool!' Then she disappeared into the bedroom, closing and locking the door after her.

'Fairlee warned me about this,' Trueman said. He sent the Sergeant out to re-enter the bedroom from the fire escape.

But as soon as the bedroom door opened we knew it was too late. Trueman looked at the inert figure on the bed. 'I suppose this will get me a black mark, but I'd rather that than another murder. She'd have used that gun all right.' He held up his hand as I moved towards the bed. 'I wouldn't, sir, if I were you,' he said quietly. I hesitated, then with a brief nod went out into the hall.

5

Richards was sitting at a table at the *L'Ecu de France* when I arrived.

'I've ordered a dozen oysters,' he said. 'Why don't you have a glass of champagne first?' He beckoned the wine waiter.

'She committed suicide,' I said, as the waiter departed.

'She'd more guts than Fairlee,' Richards said. 'He's still arguing. According to his version he knew what was going on but denied being in the organisation. He even maintains that he threatened to break off the engagement unless Barbara Day gave up the racket. He won't get away with that one at the Old Bailey. It's possible, though, that his story of killing Cordwell while in a jealous rage may be accepted. It would save him from hanging.'

'I should think it's true,' I said. 'Cordwell was battered with that ashtray, which seems to point to a fit of uncontrollable rage. Fairlee wasn't sane when we saw him in Maida Vale – although I'm not going into the witness box on his behalf.'

'You're not going into the witness box, period.' Richards said flatly. 'Ross doesn't want the department to get that sort of publicity.' He patted my arm. 'Sorry, old boy. Barbara Day was a damned attractive girl, I don't blame you for falling for her. But you've done a grand job, Frazer. Have a drink on it!'

'Bollinger . . . '49,' I said wryly reading the label on the bottle. 'A champagne to celebrate with. You finish it, Richards.'

'I'm damned if I know why,' Richards said, 'but I don't feel

like oysters and champagne today. And I understand that Ross
has another case he wants us to go to work on. Wouldn't do to
float in on the old boy, not in office hours, at any rate. I sometimes get the impression that he thinks murders that don't
take place between nine and five aren't really his department's
business. I do hope you won't find working for the Civil Service
too dull, Frazer.'

I said I'd try not to.

Two hours later as we left the restaurant Richards said: 'I
say, Frazer, you're not one of these fellows who goes in for
masculine perfume, are you?'

I sniffed the sleeve of my jacket. 'Reminds me of a girl I
once met at London Airport,' I said. 'Would you mind driving
me home first? I think I'd like to change my suit.'

'And change that handkerchief,' Richards said. 'It has lipstick on it. Ross'll take a poor view of that.'

'To hell with Ross,' I said. 'I've changed my mind. Drive
straight to Smith Square, Richards.'

Richards and I sat facing Ross, who had our reports on the
Ericson case in front of him. There was nothing in mine about
Barbara's invitation to accompany her to Cornwall. Ross closed
one of the folders and turned to me.

6

'I hope you appreciate that we have allowed you a certain
amount of latitude on this case, Frazer,' he said. 'You cleared

up the Salinger problem so neatly that I let Richards talk me into allowing you to go after Ericson. But I want you to realise that it isn't to be taken as a precedent.'

I mumbled something about being so involved that it had been difficult to withdraw.

'You were fortunate to have Richards keeping an eye on you,' said Ross severely. He closed the folders and replaced them in their file. Then he took out another folder and placed it on his desk. 'Now, about your next project . . .' he began, but was interrupted by the telephone.

The call was for Richards, who went into the adjoining office to take it. While we were waiting for him to return, Ross opened the bottom right-hand drawer of his desk and took out a cine-camera.

'You may as well have this back now,' he said. I took it and gave it a quick glance, then handed it back to him. 'This isn't mine,' I said.

'Then that explains the switching of the films,' Ross said, reaching down and producing another camera from the drawer. 'This is the one that was found with Cordwell's body.'

'Yes, they got mixed up accidentally at *De Kroon*. Cordwell's had just been returned by the police; it was stolen from his hotel on his previous visit, a month or so earlier. That would be when he took the film of the accident.'

'Yes, that's right,' Ross agreed. 'They're both the same make, and the cases are almost identical.'

'It was Vivien Gilmore who first put that idea in my head,' I went on. 'She tried to make me believe that Cordwell had picked up my camera by mistake, and then used my film to blackmail Barbara Day. It was an accidental switch all right, but Cordwell didn't need my film for blackmailing purposes – he'd already found out who Ericson was. *That's* why he was blackmailing her.'

'Perhaps it was lucky you got the wrong camera,' Ross said with a smile. 'Very occasionally, mistakes do turn out for the best, but we never accept that as an excuse in this department. However, you've made a good job of this assignment.'

I said: 'I'm glad you were proved right about Salinger, sir.'

He gave a little shrug. 'I suppose you thought I was unduly sentimental. As he was dead, what did it matter whether he was innocent or guilty? Well, it mattered to me.'

This was one of the things about Ross that ensured the full support of the men who worked for him.

Richards returned, and Ross reopened the folder on his desk.

'Now, about the next assignment, Frazer . . .'